It's Never Too
Late to Get a Life

Coming February 2006

It's Never Too Late to Be a Bridesmaid

It's Never Too Late to Get a Life

Heather Estay

AVON
TRADE

An Imprint of HarperCollinsPublishers

FIRST EDITION

Interior text designed by Elizabeth M. Glover

Library of Congress Cataloging-in-Publication Data

Estay, Heather.
 It's never too late to get a life / by Heather Estay.—1st ed.
  p. cm.
ISBN-13: 978-0-06-076250-6
ISBN-10: 0-06-076250-0
1. Divorced women—Fiction. 2. Female friendship—Fiction. 3. Mothers and daughters—Fiction. 4. Husbands—Fiction. I. Title.

PS3605.S73I7 2005
813'.6—dc22   2004021068

05 06 07 08 09 JTC/RRD 10 9 8 7 6 5 4 3 2 1

For my Mom,
who, despite all of the evidence
we've given her to the contrary,
still believes her children and grandchildren
are talented and brilliant.
I love you, Mom.

Acknowledgments

Many thanks to: Wendy Sherman for snapping me up before I had to endure too many rejection letters; Carrie Feron and Selina McLemore for gently guiding me through the publication process and for all those free books; my friends and family, whose lives supply me with material that is truly stranger than fiction; and finally, the naysayers and negative thinkers in my life who inspire me to prove them wrong!

Prologue

Obviously, I never should have gotten out of bed that morning. When the alarm went off I should have squinted one eye open, hummed a chorus of "Happy Birthday to Me," then scuttled right back under the covers. But I'm not psychic. I didn't know that my three so-called best friends were about to lure me into disaster. Nor that I'd be on the brink of ruining my reputation, losing my family, and wetting my pants while wearing a rented GI Joe costume (in which case I'm sure my deposit would have been forfeit). Of course, these same best friends did finally form the Save Angie Crisis Intervention Team to rescue me from the whole mess. But maybe I wouldn't have required rescuing if I'd simply stayed in bed that day.

Based on the hide-under-the-covers-and-it-will-go-away theory of life, I can think of many mornings I should have slept through. For instance the morning eighteen months before, when I walked into the kitchen to find my husband of twenty-six years making kissy-kissy noises into the phone.

"Bob, what are you doing?"

"I was just talking to Clarisse. You know, the Neighborhood Watch captain."

"The one who makes those Double Chocolate Cream Cheese Brownies? But why were you doing that kissy-kissy smoochie thing?"

"Well, Angie, it's probably time you knew. Clarisse and I are an item."

"An item of what?"

Perhaps you're thinking that I'm a little dense, but then you've never seen Clarisse. Clarisse looks like the before picture in an ad for *I Lost 180 Pounds in 30 Days*. Isn't there a Middle-Aged Cheating Husbands Credo somewhere that requires the other woman to be one of those nubile, half-dressed *Bay Watch* bimbos? Someone whose youth we can never recapture and whose boobs we can't afford?

"Angie, how do I put this delicately? Clarisse and I have been sleeping together for months now." *That* was delicate?

"You're having an affair with the Neighborhood Watch captain?"

"It's not an affair, Angie."

"Are you nuts, Bob? You're married to me. You're sleeping with her. That is absolutely, by definition, an affair!"

"Okay, Angie. Let's cut to the chase."

To give you a little background, Bob typically used that "let's cut to the chase" phrase to signal the end of sexual foreplay. When we were first married, I thought it was cute and kind of sexy. But over the years, as our foreplay progressed from fleeting to nonexistent, "let's cut to the chase" had become more than a little aggravating. I didn't understand the appropriateness of the phrase in this particular context until months later: I was about to get screwed.

"Angie, we've made some bad investments lately and, well, getting a divorce might be the only way to avoid bankruptcy. I'm moving in with Clarisse."

See what I mean? Definitely another one of those days I should have stayed in bed.

Chapter 1

But the morning that started it all, when hitting the snooze-forever button might have saved me, was my forty-ninth birthday (the birthday that now ranks as my worst birthday ever, far surpassing even my fourteenth, when Stanley Jackson stood me up for my own party). For the past twenty years, my birthdays have been an exhausting marathon of Happy Birthday parties. Not because I have hordes of friends who are anxious to celebrate my "special day," but because I have three best friends who refuse to celebrate it together. Why? The three of them can't stand one another, that's why.

In all the years we've known each other, I can only think of three subjects my best friends ever agreed on: a) none of them have ever liked Bob, my now ex-husband, b) none of them likes each other, and c) all of them think I am a best friend worth keeping. That's it. I don't know why they dislike each other so much. But honestly? Though these women are as dear to me as my kidneys, they really are difficult to like, even for me, their designated best friend.

Getting together with all three of them absolutely does not work. Imagine a party with Britney Spears, Sandra Day O'Conner, and Elizabeth Taylor. Maybe these women are interesting by themselves—but together? (Granted, if Liz can be best friends with Michael Jackson maybe she can party with anyone. But you get my drift.)

So every year the day begins with a Happy Birthday Breakfast, then proceeds to the Happy Birthday Lunch, and closes with the Happy Birthday Dinner, each hosted by a different best friend. It's grueling, and extremely caloric, but unavoidable. And because obviously the favored time slot is the Happy Birthday Dinner, the Happy Birthday Schedule must be rotated each year so that no best friend becomes more best than the others. Sigh . . .

On this particular birthday, Jessica had drawn the Happy Birthday Breakfast, the least desirable Happy Birthday Meal, especially for Jessica since she is *not* a morning person.

"Angie, are you absolutely sure I was supposed to be breakfast this year?" This was said with less than Jessica's usual cheerfulness, a cheerfulness which at full force can rival Glinda, Good Witch of the North. She peered out petulantly from huge, purplish sunglasses, which covered her entire face.

"Yes, Jess, I'm absolutely sure."

She had chosen a pretty little café, sunlit with lace curtains and fresh flowers, sitar music playing in the background. So very Jessica! The place was packed and noisy as we headed toward the only available table, in the center of the room.

Even in her grumpiest morning state, Jessica sparkles

like an ethereal creature from *A Midsummer Night's Dream*, never quite walking on the ground but seeming to float above it. Sunlight filtered through the wavy red hair that frames her petite, alabaster face. Those sunglasses hid inquisitive azure eyes, wide-set and deceptively innocent. Jessica is stunning, almost extraterrestrial, and incredibly unconscious of her impact on the awestruck earthlings she passes.

Being with Jessica always makes me feel heavy and clunky, though in truth, Jess and I are not too different in size and stats. Both about five-four, weighing in at 120 pounds, a pair of size fours. But Jessica is much more refined and delicate, an orange frappe to my lump of oatmeal. To top it off, despite being the proud grandma of three little girls, Jessica looks young enough to be in her late thirties. Me? I fall into the "well-preserved-for-her-age" category.

After we were seated, Jessica reached into her big flowery bag, pulled out a set of oversized headphones, and put them over her ears.

"Jess? What are you doing?"

"Oh, these!" She brightened noticeably. "These are incredible! Don't worry, I can hear everything you say. I'm listening to sound therapy tapes. They filter out the lower frequencies and enhance the higher, which opens up passages to the cortex of the brain. The result, after a hundred or so hours of listening, is reduced stress, extra energy, and improved hearing. The woman who developed them lives in Canada and . . ."

I took a deep breath and smiled. Here we go again. Jessica had experimented with every lotion, potion, mantra, organic supplement, body discipline, and diet ("It's not a diet, it's a way of life!") created. She had been Zoned, Rolfed, and Feng Shuied. And every new experience was as "absolutely incredible" as the last.

I'll admit Jessica benefits from her experiments. She's healthy and looks fantastic. But every time I see her, she has some brand-new "fabulous" discovery to share. And once she gets started talking about her latest, she can gush about it nonstop for hours. Unfortunately, Jess possesses a particularly loud and shrill voice, a voice totally incompatible with her waiflike appearance. So her gushing is about as melodic as a child's first violin lesson.

But over the years, I've learned to tune Jessica out during her infomercials. It was pleasant enough just to watch her enthuse, like turning the sound off the TV. I figured this morning's monologue would run at least twenty minutes before I'd be allowed to get a word in. So I wandered off mentally, knowing I wouldn't be missed for a while.

I started thinking about a prior birthday when Jessica had just returned from the Burning Man celebration in the desert. She had shown me a scrapbook she put together with pictures of nude mud races, exotic art, and this guy with thousands of body piercings in places that really should not have been pierced. I think she told me the guy worked as a mailman, though of course our main conversation focused on the logistics of his, uh, doing certain things and how the person who, uh, did those things with him might experience it. I was floating off, wondering whether my own mailman had such intimate piercings beneath his uniform, when Jessica's screech brought me right back to earth.

"Oh, my God, Angie! You're a virgin!"

Did I mention that Jessica has a voice as lilting as a banshee on a bad hair day? This statement was delivered in the same tone you might use for "Oh, my God! There's a lizard in my omelet!"

Perhaps not everyone in the restaurant heard her. Maybe the ninety-year-old with the hearing aid in the farthest corner missed it. But even he seemed to straighten in his seat and lean toward our table. The diners stopped dining and hushed. They had all been trained by *Oprah*, and recognized that a real-life drama was about to unfold.

"What on earth do you mean?" I hissed. As everyone knows, hissing is the universal signal that the person being hissed to was speaking too loudly and must hush. Right? Apparently, Jessica does not know this universal signal.

"I mean, since you've not had sex, you're a virgin." Jessica had not reduced her volume.

"Last I looked, I've got two children, both in their twenties, and that did not happen immaculately. I am NOT a virgin." I gave Jessica my best *"that is SO ludicrous!"* look.

My grandmother had a *"that is SO ludicrous!"* look that was a killer: eyebrow arched, lip sneering, nostrils slightly flared. Grandma's look could stop traffic or prevent a volcano from erupting. I know for sure it stopped Grandpa from smoking cigars and it stopped me, at fifteen, from going out with Danny Bernardini, the Bad Boy of the tenth grade. It's an incredibly powerful look, and I had spent hours practicing it in front of my mirror. If I'd had even a tenth of my grandmother's talent at *"that is SO ludicrous!"* I would have stopped Jessica dead in her tracks. But I didn't. My look always came across more like *"oooo, too much lemon!"*

"Oh, Angie, don't you know anything? Energetically, if you have not had sex for over a year, you become a virgin again!" I swear the ninety-year-old across the room took out his hearing aid, tapped it a few times, replaced it, and edged his chair closer to our table.

"Jessica, that's ridiculous."

"But you haven't, have you?"

"Haven't what?"

"Had sex in over a year."

The restaurant was incredibly quiet. Waitresses had appeared from nowhere to fill coffee cups and water glasses in our vicinity that clearly did not need filling. Not only had all conversation stopped, but all chewing, rustling, and breathing had stopped as well.

I figured I had two choices. I could either A) strangle Jessica with her headphone wires in front of seventy-five spellbound witnesses or B) take the chance that a brief, direct answer would shut her up. Through a total lack of imagination and with much reluctance, I chose option B.

"Well, okay, so actually, no. I haven't. I haven't had sex in over a year. Satisfied?"

"Of *course* I'm not satisfied! This is awful!" Jessica's volume was increasing, perhaps to include folks across town who could not yet hear our exchange.

Have you ever wondered what could possibly possess people to show up on Sally Jessy Raphael or Dr. Phil and reveal intimate, humiliating secrets in front of zillions of strangers? They were probably conned into it by a kooky best friend who invited them to a Happy Birthday Breakfast.

"Angie, lack of sex can be a serious health risk. It's been proven that frequent orgasms can reduce the risk of osteoporosis and other menopausal symptoms. And you are definitely heading into menopause, right?"

Oh, goody, now we were announcing my menopausal condition to the world. We live in California, for heaven's sake! Where's an earthquake when you need one?

"Angie, we can't let this . . . this . . . premature, unnatural celibacy go on! We have to do something about this." Was it too late for me to go back to the strangling-with-headphones option?

I am an extraordinarily patient person. I raised one kid who would not eat anything green, red, or yellow for the first thirteen years of his life, and another who, until age nine, had to hear *Goodnight Moon* a minimum of three times every single night before she would fall asleep. For twenty-six years, I lived with a man who channel surfed for hours without ever actually landing on a channel. I've endured PTA meetings (main topic: whether cupcakes should be banned from lunch boxes as potential health hazards) and business meetings (main topic: whether we should replan the project plan we just planned and if so, what was the plan to plan that replanning). Maybe Mother Teresa could score higher on the patience meter than I can, but did Mother Teresa ever give driving lessons to a fifteen-year-old with four quarts of testosterone coursing through his veins? I don't think so.

I started my deep breathing, the kind that helps you endure childbirth and rein in homicidal urges that might otherwise earn you the death penalty (and a six-figure book contract). I reached over and gently removed Jessica's headphones. I adopted the singsong voice that always works when calming two-year-olds in tantrums and lunatics on rampages.

"Jessica, I appreciate your concern. But *we* are perfectly happy the way *we* are. And even if *we* weren't, *we* are not even dating."

That was true. Neither of us was dating. Me because I was too frightened, lacking in self-esteem, and out of practice to 'get out there.' And Jessica because she was happily (for the most part) engaged to and living with a very nice man, which means she wasn't technically dating any longer.

"And therefore, Jess, *we* are not in a position to do anything about this issue. So, end of subject, okay?"

Jessica scrunched up her nose in deep concentration; it's not much of a nose, but it was a very deep concentration. Our restaurant audience held its breath. Waitresses, having refilled all possible liquids in our immediate vicinity, gave up the pretense and simply hovered.

"No. It's not okay, Angie." Was there a silent cheer throughout the restaurant? Did the applause sign light up? I looked up at the closest gaping waitress and glared. She moved, but just barely out of glare range.

"Angie, here's what I seriously, seriously, *seriously* think." Jessica paused dramatically to let me know that this is what she seriously, seriously, *seriously* thought about it all. "You need to have a One Night Stand."

Okay, so like most of us, I've gotten plenty of advice through my life, maybe 75 percent of it unsolicited. And a lot of it has not been exactly Dear Abby quality. But this? This set a standard for really rotten advice that would be hard to match in future years.

"Jessica? Are you nuts? What would possess you to recommend a One Night Stand? That is so tawdry!" My vocabulary definitely improves under stress. "Do you think so little of me that you would have me debase myself and do . . . do . . . that? Am I no longer your best friend?" A low blow perhaps, but she deserved it.

"Angie, let me put this to you simply." Jessica's pixie chin was set resolutely; her voice was steady, certain, deadly. "Your chakras are totally blocked. You will never find true happiness until you become unblocked. Sometimes, it requires dramatic action to burst through barriers, to become unblocked. You need to have a One Night Stand."

I didn't look up. I couldn't look up. But if I had, I am sure I would have seen the entire restaurant nodding in sage agreement: *Yep, she's right. One Night Stand. The only reasonable solution.*

"Angie, remember how we were in the sixties and seventies? Before we became matrons and mommies and Republicans? We were free and enjoyed our sensuality and . . ."

"Oh, you mean before we became aware of AIDS and social diseases and psychopathic killers preying on unsuspecting women! Jessica, grow up!" I was getting angry by then, raising my volume, discretion out the window. No more hissing! In truth, much of my indignation was because, well, I didn't remember the sixties and seventies. Oh, I was there all right. But not *there* there, know what I mean? While everyone else was experiencing free love and mind-expanding drugs and wild sex, I was, um, studying. It's one of the more embarrassing secrets of my life.

Jessica was not dissuaded. "Oh, for heaven's sake! You'll obviously take precautions. Look, I'm your best friend. Would I tell you to do something that I didn't absolutely know for sure would be good for you? You don't want to become frigid, do you? End up as one of those mean old spinsters who goes around murdering grocery store clerks?"

Every once in a while a conversation with Jessica will take a particularly bizarre turn. She is one of the few people I've met who actually reads and remembers stories from the *National Enquirer*. I am smart enough not to question her hypothesis that a grocery store clerk was murdered because some old lady didn't go out and get laid; that conversation would go straight *Through the Looking Glass*. I tried a different tack.

"Jessica, look, maybe you're right. Maybe I do need some, uh, intimacy with a man. But I really don't even know anyone who would be a candidate. So, can we drop this?"

"Well, Angie, a One Night Stand doesn't have to be with someone you know." The ninety-year-old sat up in his seat, ready to volunteer.

Chapter 2

My Happy Birthday Breakfast lasted longer than usual, me arguing for my virtue, Jessica insisting on wanton sex as the cure for my constipated kundalini. By the time I could escape, I was running late for my Happy Birthday Lunch. Happy Birthday Lunch this year was with Gwen. Gwen the Calm, Cool, Collected. Gwen the Studied and Correct. I craved a dose of Gwen after that breakfast with Jessica!

I flew through the restaurant door, disheveled and harried, to find Gwen as always, perfectly poised and polished. She wore a suit in a sage-colored silk, custom-tailored for her tall, angular frame; her sleek twenty-four-karat earrings and matching necklace clearly cost more than my minivan. Gwen's short black hair was cut in a chic, upswept style, defying the laws of gravity and hair spray, and her sophisticated makeup emphasized arched eyebrows and high cheekbones. Everything about Gwen says confidence, power. You might take her to be a CEO or a US senator or, as it turns out she is, a successful attorney. In small-town Sacramento, Gwen is noticeable for her big-city style.

In contrast, my so-called style is based on whatever happens to be clean and ironed, whatever I can throw on during that inevitable last-minute scramble before leaving the house. As far as I can tell, Gwen never scrambles getting dressed or doing anything else for that matter. That day, I wore khaki slacks with loafers and a light blue cotton shirt with a navy blue sweater over my shoulders, the Lands-End-Too-Lazy-to-Figure-It-Out look. My hair was clean but it just slumped over my head as if too exhausted to do anything else. My makeup, as usual, was a slapdash job, and I had forgotten to use blush on my not-so-prominent cheekbones. Predictably, my lipstick had been chewed off hours before. (I've never believed that consistently perfect lipstick is a matter of superior product or expert application. I'm convinced that it's a genetic gift. You either have good lipstick genes, or you don't. I don't; women like Gwen do.)

If Jessica makes me feel coarse and cloddish, Gwen always makes me feel dowdy and unkempt. Why would I choose such friends, you ask? Well, actually, maybe I didn't. Maybe they chose me, a convenient foil. Isn't that why Dean Martin chose Jerry Lewis? Lucy chose Ethel? Nixon chose Ford? I tucked in my shirt, pushed back my lazy hair, and rolled up my sleeve to cover the strawberry jam stain, a souvenir from breakfast.

Ordinarily, I won't discuss my best friends with one another, not wanting to inflame their mutual antipathy. But that day I was dying to tell Gwen, levelheaded, feminist Gwen, about Jessica's outrageous suggestion. However, I knew I'd have to be patient because Gwen can be very high-maintenance in restaurants.

We were seated at a small table in the middle of the dining room. Would they mind moving us to the window? Oh, there seems to be a draft here. How about the table at the other window? Yes, it's a table for four, but would they mind terribly . . . ?

As soon as we were situated, I hurried to order first, bracing myself for the inevitable. Our waiter, who had introduced himself as George, turned to Gwen with a smile. Poor innocent man!

"And for you, ma'am?"

"I'll have the Caesar salad with chicken." George smiled his approval. "And please see that the chicken is warmed ever so slightly before it goes in the salad."

"Certainly." George was smooth.

"And rather than Parmesan, could you please use Romano? I don't want the Romano mixed into the salad. I like it on top, not too much, but not all mixed in."

"Of course." No hesitation.

"I see you also have a spinach salad?"

George paused imperceptibly. "Uh, yes, ma'am we do."

"Perfect. Then you could put just a touch of fresh spinach in with the romaine. Just a touch, not too much." George's confidence wavered slightly.

"Yes. Um, of course we could do that."

"And I don't want the rolls with it."

"Of course. No rolls."

"But, George, would you have dry, unsalted crackers instead? Something like matzos would be fine."

"Matzos?"

"But no breadsticks. And no sesame seeds."

"No sesame seeds?"

"With unsalted, whipped butter on the side."

"Whipped?" George was definitely beginning to crack. I gave him my most reassuring look and started humming "You've Got a Friend."

"And, George, would you have a flavored iced tea? Not raspberry but anything else would be fine. Except no caffeine and no sugar." George nodded mutely, seriously questioning his career choice by then.

"If not, I'll just have bottled water, sparkling, but only if it's domestic. With lime on the side, please."

As George turned to leave, I gave him a big encouraging smile, which he did not return.

"Oh, and George? Could you make sure that the Caesar dressing is not made with anchovies? If it is, I'll have to start from scratch and order something else entirely." George's body deflated, and he looked at me desperately. I knew that look. I had seen it months ago during a tuna fish sandwich order that had left a waitress across town in tears. George fled to the kitchen.

With the ordeal of ordering completed, I vented my frustration about Jessica and her suggestion. I gave Gwen a spirited, detailed, and only slightly exaggerated reenactment of the entire conversation at breakfast. The only interruption came when George, unwilling to face the firing squad alone, returned with the chef in tow to discuss Gwen's alternatives to the anchovy-tainted dressing.

"Honestly, Gwen, what kind of friend would come up with such a harebrained scheme? Can you imagine?" I waited for Gwen to burst forth in rousing support. Nothing. She continued to chew her anchovy-free salad thoughtfully. Maybe I should have concluded with *I rest my case.* "Well? Gwen, are you listening?"

"Angie, though I think the basis of Jessica's underlying argument is completely absurd, she just may have stumbled on the correct conclusion."

"What?"

I was stunned. I could disregard a suggestion from Jessica. Jessica isn't dumb, but her out-of-the-box thinking often wanders into *The Twilight Zone.* But Gwen is really smart. She and I had gone to Stanford together, which is not significant in itself. I mean I, like a lot of my classmates, am just smart-ish. No particular brilliance or genius, maybe just a vague appreciation for literature and an enhanced ability to follow the dialogue on *The West Wing.* But Gwen has a mind that is daunting. It was rumored that she had set some kind of record on her LSAT scores (though she's never verified it) and her law degree is from Harvard. She had clerked for a Supreme Court justice, then built an employment law practice in Sacramento that is recognized nationally. Not that any of that makes her infallible in the personal advice category. But it's hard to ignore someone whose IQ is higher than her body weight.

"Angie, consider what you have been through. Your husband left you broke and for a woman with the body of a sea cow and the face of a Chinese shar-pei. Your self esteem must be in the toilet. You must look in the mirror and wonder 'What on earth is wrong with me?' You must question your own attractiveness, sexuality, femininity."

Actually, I hadn't really questioned all of those things—but I was beginning to.

"So this might be the perfect way to gain back your power, the very act of sex and with an anonymous male to symbolize all the males in your life who have ever betrayed you."

"Anonymous? I can't even know his name?"

"Don't be dense! Anonymous as in someone that you don't really have a relationship with, that you don't really care for."

"Gwen, I can't do that! It's too . . . too coldhearted, too callous for me. I can't imagine hurting a guy's feelings that way."

"You are truly lame sometimes, Angie." She was clearly exasperated with me. I know Gwen works very hard to avoid being condescending with others (though, as brilliant as she is, it would naturally be her right). But sometimes, when faced with supreme idiocy, she can't help herself. This was one of those times.

"A man who gets a chance to have unencumbered sex will feel absolutely blessed, not wounded. Don't you know anything?"

Well, actually, no. Apparently I didn't. But I was not yet ready to give up the fight. "Gwen, I thought you were a feminist. As a good feminist, how can you justify sending me off to become some man's sex object?"

Gwen's eyebrow arched at me severely, and I knew I had grasped at the wrong straw. "Angie, when you were married to Bob," the way Gwen said it, *Bob* sounded suspiciously like *vermin*, "you were positioned as an 'object.' What I'm talking about is a sexual encounter between two equal human beings, exchanging pleasure with no chains, no obligations. Don't you remember any of Germaine Greer's writings? Or Jong's *Fear of Flying?* One of the key tenets of the feminist movement is that sexuality and power are intertwined, and . . ."

I had never seen Gwen in court, but now knew why she was worth $475 per hour, plus expenses. Within two minutes (a mere $15.83's worth), she had me feeling that a One Night Stand was not only politically correct, but perhaps my sacred duty to further the evolution of womanhood.

I don't think you'd define me as an ardent feminist. I was more ardent in the late sixties, when we were busy being "as capable as men." Fortunately, we soon realized that "as capable as men" was a relatively low standard that didn't require much effort on our parts (except for long-distance spitting and crotch adjusting, skills that still elude most of us). What did and still does require effort are the issues that remain unresolved: equal pay and opportunity, exploitation and abuse of women, and the great toilet seat dispute. When I'm in position to affect those first two issues, I do so with enthusiasm. But I can't build up much steam for debates on toilet seats or parity in housework. And given how rampant and entertaining male bashing has become, I'm willing to overlook a few sexist remarks now and then. I guess that makes me a lethargic feminist, too lazy to sweat the small stuff.

"So, Angie, I can't tell you what to do." Gwen had just spent twenty minutes clearly telling me exactly what to do. "But you really should think about whether you want fear and outdated convention to determine the course of your life. Or whether you are ready to express the essence of your full feminine power, your true being."

Oh, is that all? In that case, my true being wanted a little birthday cake, and I needed to express my essence by finding the ladies' room. I'd had a few too many Happy Birthday iced teas.

Chapter 3

I arrived home early that evening, emotionally bruised and battered from my first two Happy Birthday celebrations. Marie, the best friend scheduled for Happy Birthday Dinner, was waiting in my driveway. Actually, she was waiting in *her* driveway, which also happened to be my driveway. I didn't live with Marie, but *behind* Marie and her husband Jack in their tiny studio guesthouse, my personal little postdivorce homeless shelter.

For the uninitiated, let me explain about the division of marital property in a divorce situation. You (and your accountant) and the man who lied about "for better or worse" (and his accountant) get together and make up two lists: 1) Unencumbered Assets (in our case, a very brief list) and 2) Debts to Be Paid or Else (a painfully long list). It doesn't matter who bought what or who earned what because during the years of "until death do us part" you are considered one fiscal entity by the State. Anyway, the State throws these two lists into a Cuisinart and divides the mess between the two divorcing parties based on some formula that only the State can comprehend. In short, I ended up with 50 percent of nothing and 50 percent of a whole lot of debt.

Bob (shall we say to his credit?) paid off a large portion of our debt, with the assistance of the generous and generously proportioned Clarisse. It turns out that Clarisse is loaded. Her dearly departed husband had died of a heart attack last year while getting a "physical therapy treatment" in a local motel room, leaving the lovely, cellulite-laden Clarisse with a bazillion dollars and several weeks of indelicate (and quite humorous) coverage in the local press. Remind me to feel sorry for Clarisse someday.

So Bob's portion of the debt was handled. But to clear what was left, it became obvious (through the persistent nudging of my creditors and my accountant, Marvin) that selling the house was my only alternative. Arrgh! My house, my *home* for more than twenty-five years. I had lived there longer than any place in my entire life. My kids had been born there, had grown up there. In my more rational moments, I knew that the house wouldn't fit my new lifestyle as a middle-aged divorcée living alone. But there were so many memories, so much of *me* in that place! It was like moving away from your childhood home for the first time and knowing you'll never go back—only this time, I had been kicked out.

But I had no other option. During the agony of that decision and the numbness of "What next?" Marie had stepped up to offer me and my two beagles, Spud and Alli, a home. For the last six months we had lived behind Marie and Jack. It was a blessing.

The arrangement worked out incredibly well. Marie/Jack

and I respected each other's privacy while enjoying each other's company. Marie popped over for a glass of wine and a chat after work every couple of days or so. Jack periodically invited me to admire the latest addition to his model railroad. Often they invited me to join them for dinner or to listen to some new jazz band Jack had discovered. And yet I could go for days at a time without seeing either of them. It was perfect. We were roommates with plenty of room.

So there Marie stood on her/my driveway looking like a colorful earth goddess. Standing five-six, she still appears statuesque due to her ballerina-perfect posture. Marie has one of those curvy, rounded, huggable bodies, the antithesis of the sticklike models of the last few decades. That night she wore a long-sleeved sarong-style dress that flowed to her ankles in deep reds and purples.

Marie is striking from a distance, but the impact of her womanly allure doesn't hit until you get up close. An American Gina Lollobrigida, Marie exudes an earthy sensuality though I can't pinpoint exactly how she does it. Maybe it's her eyes, gypsy eyes Jack calls them, or the thick dark hair that falls to her shoulders in natural waves. Or maybe it's her deep, husky voice or her slow, syncopated walk (I tried that walk once, and it threw my back out for a week). Whatever it is, it isn't accomplished with a lot of effort or artifice; it's just simply who Marie is. Men of all types, shapes, and ages go goofy and gaga around her. Next to Marie, I feel like Mary Martin playing Peter Pan—completely genderless.

"I fed the pups for you. Are you ready to go?"

"Oh, Marie, I can't tell you how ready I am! This has really been a day!"

We lifted ourselves into her ancient Land Rover and headed off toward midtown Sacramento. It was mid-September, the summer-to-autumn transition time when our days are still in the eighties but the temperature drops to the low fifties by early evening. We drove to an Italian restaurant, the kind of friendly, cozy place only Marie seems to find. We didn't make a stir when we entered; we didn't need to find the perfect table; we just sat down. What a relief to be with Marie!

"Okay, Marie. Today two of my other so-called friends insisted that I have a One Night Stand. Their arguments included, but were not limited to, opening up my cosmic energy centers and reasserting my essential feminine power. What do you think?"

Marie just looked at me. That's what Marie does. She never says anything quickly without considering whatever the heck it is that Marie considers before speaking. I've learned not to rush her and not to be too uncomfortable under her penetrating stare, a stare that scrutinizes my every twitching nostril hair.

"Hmmm. Wow, Angie. Interesting. What do *you* think?"

That was all the prompting I needed.

"I think they are totally crazy! I can't even imagine having sex with a new man! I've been with the same man for twenty-six years. I know how to 'do it' with Bob, but how do you 'do it' with someone you hardly know? I'm not totally inexperienced, but the last time I had a lover other than Bob, I was in my twenties.

"And I'm forty-nine for God's sake! I'm all wrinkly and

saggy, and, if I was going to cruise for dudes, it should have been two decades ago! A husband *has* to accept your cellulite and extra moles and droopy boobs. But a new lover? Why would he want someone as 'used up' as I am?

"Plus I have two adult children. What would Tyler and Jenna think of all this? They know me as good old Mom, stable and reliable, baking cookies, driving a minivan, and darning their socks. Okay, so I don't really know how to darn socks, but you get the gist. How would they deal with their mother becoming a wanton and wild woman out on the circuit?"

My tirade had taken on a life of its own by that point. My eloquence is unmatched when it comes to describing my inadequacies and defending my God-given right to be cowardly. I gulped some wine and a breath of air and continued.

"Besides that, I've got two beagles who sleep with me. There are dog hairs all over the place, and I sleep in old T-shirts. My lumpy old mattress is the same one I had when the kids were little and not yet potty trained. So I'm sure, if I could smell it anymore, it has a slight 'Eau Baby Pee' scent to it. Hardly romantic.

"And I don't even know what safe sex is exactly. I mean, I know what it is, but I don't know how you, like, start the conversation. 'Hey, Mr. X, got a condom on you? Any STDs lately?' Are we supposed to schedule blood tests and urinalysis before we leap into bed? Doesn't that kind of kill the 'wild abandon' part of it?"

I was certain that I was winning this argument. But somehow, I wasn't feeling good about the victory. Marie's face remained impassive. I swear she hadn't blinked once since we sat down.

"Really, Marie, it's completely overwhelming. It's just too late for me to get into the whole mating game again. And even if it wasn't, I don't need just sex. I need someone who will care for me and love me and stay with me for the long run."

I ran out of steam and started to tear up.

"Oh, and I snore."

Marie refilled my wineglass and stared at me for a really long time, even by Marie standards. I blew my nose on the red napkin that matched the checkered tablecloth (Now, what is the etiquette here? Do you just keep blowing on that napkin and warn the waiter that it is now a biohazard when he clears the table? Or do you tuck it in your purse? Is napkin stealing a punishable crime if it's done for public health safety reasons?)

"So, Angie, what I heard was this: You are frightened about moving out of your comfort zone. You have some anxiety about your age and attractiveness. You are worried about what other people, especially your children, might think. You have some housekeeping issues. And you need some tutoring on dating etiquette. Did I get it right?"

"Uh-huh." My lip was quivering. I took another sip of wine. I was *not* having a happy Happy Birthday.

"Okay, so any of that can be resolved. But you know something, Angie? I think the most important thing you said was that you wanted someone to cherish you and love you for the long run."

"Uh-huh." My lip was quivering at full throttle, and the tears were streaming. I do not cry pretty, I cry ugly. My nose gets red, my mascara runs, and my mouth gets all weird and crinkly. I happen to know all of this because I'd had frequent opportunities to watch myself cry over the last eighteen months.

So this epitomizes why Marie fits into the "difficult" category along with my other best friends. More often than not, a conversation with Marie brings me to tears. I'm sure I could go blithely through my life without once encountering myself, confronting myself, or questioning Life's Bigger Issues. But then I'll get together with Marie, and we'll dive right into some concern I didn't even know I had. She's a submarine, unable merely to float on the surface. She's much happier at soul-wrenching depth and always draws me down there with her. It's like having your own personal therapist. Marie is candid and insightful, and though that might sound good, sometimes I would just prefer to paddle around in the shallows, not "discover" myself and ruin my makeup.

"So, Angie, you're at one of those crossroads, aren't you? Nobody can tell you what you should do. But I will tell you that my first date with Jack was a One Night Stand."

"Excuse me?"

"The night I met Jack, my date was late, and so I was waiting in the bar. Jack approached me, and he was the sexiest man I had ever seen. He was so hot, I just couldn't resist him!"

Now I really like Jack, but I doubt he'll ever be voted Stud Muffin of the Month. Out of all the men who were chasing Marie, Jack was the one who lit up her Christmas tree?

"I ditched my date—can you believe it?—and went

home with Jack. I'd never done something like that before, but I just knew that sex with him would be phenomenal, and, Angie, I was absolutely right. He was, and is, terrific in bed."

"Frankly, Marie, this is more information than I really need to know."

"Angie, you're too funny!" I am? "Anyway, I honestly assumed it would be just a One Night Stand like Gwen and Jessica are talking about. I thought Jack and I would get it on, have one great night of sex together, and that would be the end of it."

I was having a hard time absorbing all of this; it seemed so out of character for both of them. Jack is somewhere in his late sixties, funny and smart, a retired judge, definitely not my image of the bottom feeders who cruise bars seeking women. And as a couple, Marie and Jack are so extraordinarily romantic and compatible. The tacky beginning she described just didn't seem to fit.

Marie and Jack have the type of marriage we all dreamed we would have, but upon waking found that we didn't. They never bicker or snipe at one another, which alone must qualify them for marital sainthood, but it's not just a question of being polite. They are absolutely enamored and utterly fascinated with one another. They laugh at each other's jokes and listen to one another's stories. They hold hands at the movies and while walking down the street. He brings her flowers for no reason, and she absolutely lights up when he enters the room. They've been together for ten years, a second marriage for both of them, and they act as if they are still on their honeymoon. Pretty nauseating, huh? Actually with them, it's inspirational.

"It obviously turned out to be much more with Jack. I feel totally loved and cherished, like I found my true soul mate that night." Marie's eyes, normally intense anyway, were particularly impassioned, and for that brief moment, I experienced the power of her feelings for Jack. "I made a bold, spontaneous, and probably stupid move. But because of it, I stumbled into all of those things you say you want. So, Angie, I guess we never know what we're going to find when we open up to a new experience in life. Like that 'box of chocolates' saying."

"Who said that? Gomer Pyle?"

"Forrest Gump. Have some more wine, Angie."

Chapter 4

I jumped out of the birthday cake, wearing nothing but a thin veneer of goose bumps. The rowdy crowd hooted and hollered as my bump-and-grind music started to play. I spotted Gwen, Jessica, and Marie in the throng. "Shake it, Angie!" they screamed. Shake what? I looked down at little bits of frosting nestled in the craters of my cellulite. The starting bell rang, letting me know I had to start dancing or else. I was paralyzed. Shake what? The bell rang again. It rang again, then again . . . I scrambled for the phone.

"Mom? I didn't wake you up, did I?"

"No, of course not, Tyler, it's almost, uh, 6:00 A.M. I've been up for hours." I struggled to sound chipper and not as hungover as I felt. How many carafes of vino did Marie and I polish off last night? I checked under the covers to make sure there was no residual frosting stuck in my belly button.

"Well, Happy Birthday, Mom! Did you have fun yesterday? Did the aunties behave themselves? Did you get the flowers I sent you?"

"Uh, a) not exactly, b) not at all, and, c) yes, I got the flowers, and they're absolutely beautiful, honey. That was so thoughtful of you." Tyler's huge bouquet was larger than my kitchen and contained all of my favorite flowers, none of which were in season in September. Who but Tyler could have found them? Who but Tyler would have remembered which ones were my favorites? I adore this kid.

"Mom, I've got news." Tyler's typically controlled tone was edged with excitement. "When I finish my project here next month, I'll be coming back to Sacramento to clerk for Judge Bennett in the U.S. District Court."

"You're kidding! Oh, Tyler, that's great!" I sat up quickly, much too quickly for the wine-soaked gray matter inside my head, which slammed against the front of my skull in an escape attempt.

"It's not certain yet. They've had a last-minute opening. I've gone through all of the preliminary interviews, and they say it's in the bag. But I still have to interview with Judge Bennett herself, and I hear she's pretty tough. But if I get it, I could start immediately, and they'd arrange time so I can study for the California Bar in February."

"Judge Bennett is a she?"

"Sure why not? I think she's about your age and graduated Harvard Law. I'll bet Auntie Gwen knows her." I made a note to quiz Gwen at the first opportunity. Not that I would interfere or ask Gwen to use her influence, if she has any, with Judge Bennett. Unless of course, Gwen really, really insists on using her influence, in which case it would be rude to deny her the pleasure of doing so, don't you think?

"We have to finish and submit the article in five weeks, Mom, so I should be home by the end of October, just in time for Halloween."

"Then you'll be here for the holidays, too. Tyler, this is wonderful! I am so excited!" And I really was excited, but the anxiety of a not-normal Thanksgiving and Christmas flared up quickly. Last Thanksgiving was weird, the kids trotting back and forth between having turkey with me and visiting their father, the turkey who had filed for divorce. Christmas was even more of a strain, but at least the kids and I still celebrated in our old home. But this year? I love my cute little studio, but it's so small I can see both the shower and the refrigerator from my bed. How could I serve us Thanksgiving turkey on a table that could be mistaken for a TV tray? Would we hang Christmas stockings on the ceiling fan? Tyler would have to lay out his sleeping bag on the beagles' bed or in the bathtub. Within a nanosecond, my maternal worry engine had revved into overdrive. But Tyler, as usual, was ahead of me.

"Mom, I know this year will be different for all of us. But I was thinking we could start some new traditions, like going out for Thanksgiving dinner rather than staying at home. We could rent a cabin at Tahoe for a couple of days at Christmas, or . . ."

Tyler's optimism and self-confidence were contagious. We chatted about his studies for the bar, about my work, about life in general, carefully avoiding any discussion of his dad.

"Well, I should go to the gym before hitting the library again. I love you, Mom."

"I love you too, honey." My kids and I always close this way based on the *If you get hit by a truck, what do you want your last words to be?* theory of life that my mom taught me.

I leaped out of bed (actually it was more of a stagger—how many carafes did we drink?) and danced (stumbled) the ten steps from my bed to the kitchen. Spud and Alli, my Wonder Beagles whose breakfast was overdue by at least seven minutes, gazed at me piteously, which is a pretty standard beagle gaze. As I prepared their breakfast, Spud sat at attention, shaking with anticipation, watching carefully in case I dribbled any precious kibble for him to salvage. Alli bounced up and down, ears flying merrily as she launched herself with abandon to counter height in her Pre-Meal Happy Dance.

Still glowing from Tyler's call, I remembered mother/son conversations of the past. For instance, six-year-old Tyler approaching me as I made dinner:

"Mom, I've decided what I want to be when I grow up."

"Oh? A fireman? A cowboy?"

"No, Mom. Firemen are always getting burned, and cowboys have to sleep with cattle and cattle stink. So I'm going to be an attorney and present cases to the Supreme Court."

"Really? And why do you want to do that, Tyler?"

"Because I want to be like Through Good Marshall."

"Honey, I think you mean Thurgood."

"Yep, him. He's cool. He can argue smarter than any of the other guys, and he made them change some very, very bad, bad laws. He's a Supreme Court justice now, but I don't want to do that."

"Really, honey? Why not?"

"Because then they'd make me wear a dress."

By age eight and a half, Tyler's future plans were becoming more solid:

"Mom, you've probably been worrying about how we'll pay for law school."

"Well, honey, I . . ."

"And if I'm going be a lawyer at the Supreme Court, I need to go to a very good law school, and I think that is very expensive."

"So, Tyler, how expensive do you think that might be?"

"Maybe a million dollars. What do you think, Mom? Should I try to get a paper route or maybe mow lawns to earn the money?"

"Honey, go to the dictionary and look up the word 'scholarship.' "

"What's a scholarship?"

"It's money they will give you to go to law school if you are exceptionally smart, get outstanding grades, and get extraordinary test scores."

"Oh, okay. That'll be easier than mowing lawns. Mom, did you know that most American presidents were lawyers?"

By age eleven, Tyler had mapped out a detailed road map to his goal:

"Mom, I need to learn to speak Latin."

"Why, honey? I don't think anyone speaks Latin anymore."

"But a lot of laws are written with Latin words. I think you have to speak it to be a lawyer."

"Tyler, honestly, I know a lot of idiot attorneys, and I am certain that they do not speak Latin."

"But they don't appear before the Supreme Court, do they?"

"Well, no."

"So? When do you think I can start learning it? Mom, have you ever heard of Clarence Darrow?"

Tyler, age sixteen:

"Tyler, aren't you going to ask someone to the dance?"

"No, Mom. I've got to study."

"Honey, your dad and I are worried about you."

"Yeah, Dad's probably worried that I'm gay or something."

"Look, Tyler, I don't know what your dad thinks. But frankly, honey, I don't care what you are as long as you're happy. You just don't seem to be having much fun."

"Mom, to get where I want to go I need to stay on this grind until after law school. There's plenty of time for fun after that. And I do like girls, a lot actually. So I've decided that dating would be too distracting right now. But don't tell Dad that. Let's let him sweat it out, okay? By the way, Mom, did you know that Gandhi was an attorney?"

And now we were coming to the end of Tyler's very long, hard journey. Neither his dad nor I have such organized ambition, so I'm not sure what mutant chromosome ignited it in Tyler. But I was proud of him and thrilled that he would be coming home.

Tyler hadn't lived in Sacramento since he left for college seven years ago, attending Columbia for his undergraduate years, then Georgetown for law school. He had stayed after graduation to take the District of Columbia Bar exam in July. After that, some of his professors invited him to assist them with an article for the *Georgetown Law Journal*, quite an honor apparently. He seems to like it back East, but I had hated the thought that he might never return to California. I've tried to be good at the maternal letting-go process. The kids were both encouraged to be independent and self-reliant as they grew up. And when they were ready to move out and start their own lives, I applauded them and helped them pack. The problem is that I really like my offspring, and I'd much prefer to have them be independent and self-reliant within driving distance (which is not to say within *Mom, can you do my laundry* distance).

The Wonder Beagles and I climbed back into bed humming "Our boy's coming home" to the tune of "Home, Home on the Range." We snuggled down under the covers—beagles are world-class snugglers—for our postbreakfast nap. How many carafes of wine *did* we drink last night?

It's Christmas. Tyler, Jenna, and I are huddled around a candle in a dark, little shack. Bob stands over us like a portly Ebenezer Scrooge. "You will get no Double Chocolate Cream Cheese Brownies for Christmas!" he yells. "But couldn't we have just a crumb, sir?" we beg. We hear Santa Claus ho-ho-hoing at the door. It's Clarisse with a phony beard carrying a big bag of Brussels sprouts. Her humongous hips get stuck in the doorway. Bob tries to yank her out while the kids and I try not to laugh. Santa's reindeer are outside, butting Clarisse's massive rump with their horns to push her through, their bells jangling and jangling and . . .

"Angie? Did I wake you? What are you doing in bed? It's almost 7:00 A.M. You sound awful."

"Just recovering from a little too much birthday, Lilah."

"Well, Happy Birthday, my dear. I suppose you spent it with those wacky friends of yours."

"Yes, I did." I grinned to myself. Lilah could easily fit in with my wacky friends.

"So how are you? How are the kids? What's the news? By the way, I just talked to that good-for-nothing ex-husband of yours."

That good-for-nothing ex-husband of mine happens to be Lilah's son. She's my mother-in-law, not my *ex*-mother-in-law as she will explain to anyone who happens to question it: "For Heaven's sake! I kept up with my side of the bargain. Just because that worthless son of mine reneged on his vows, doesn't mean I'm an *ex* anything!" Talking to Lilah can get tricky. She's allowed to vilify, malign, disparage, and generally diss Bob, and she often does so with sidesplitting wit. But woe be to the person who agrees with her, laughs at her observations, or says anything negative about her Baby Boy. I clamped my lips between my teeth in preparation for keeping my comments and my chuckles to myself.

"Honestly, I don't know what that idiot son of mine was thinking. To hook up with that cow! Granted she's rich, which makes her a cash cow, but still, it's ridiculous."

"Hmmm." I giggled behind my clenched teeth.

"I mean, you're no Christie Brinkley, my dear, but you are a very attractive woman considering your age and all.

39

The only thing that woman has over you is her Double Chocolate Cream Cheese Brownies, which really are superior."

"Hmmm."

"Out of loyalty to you, I swear I will never ask that woman for the recipe. You don't happen to have it, do you, dear?"

"I'm afraid not, Lilah."

"Not important. Anyway, the whole situation is disgusting. To imagine my son fancying himself a gigolo, a boy toy! My God, he's got a forty-four-inch waist, spindly legs, and more hair in his ears than on his head. And I've never known a man who could stink up a bathroom worse than Bob. You need special breathing apparatus to go in after one of his visits to the commode."

"Hmmm." My lips weren't strong enough to muffle my chortles; I bit down on my knuckle.

"And he snores like a motorcycle with no muffler. Not that you are perfect, my dear. I wouldn't classify you as the ultimate Donna-Reed–type wife and mother. What was her husband's name? Mr. Reed?"

"Gosh, I don't know, Lilah."

"Whatever. My point is that you don't exactly maintain a Martha Stewart household or a Jane Fonda body, do you, dear?"

"That's true, Lilah." I managed to spit this out before cramming the pillow in my mouth.

"Angie dear, did you ever try livening up the marriage a bit? Like greeting Bob at the door some evening wearing only Saran Wrap? I read about that somewhere. I'm not sure how it works exactly, but they say it's very sexy."

"Hmmm. Sounds like it." I tried to imagine myself, or anyone else for that matter, draped seductively in plastic wrap.

"But that's all water under the bridge now, isn't it? In fact, I know that your marriage had been a leaky boat for quite a while, my dear. But that idiot son of mine turned it into the *Titanic*. At least on the *Titanic*, the captain let women and children off first. He didn't have the SS *Clarisse* waiting in the wings to bail him out like Bob did." Tears were streaming down my face and my stomach hurt. Do you know how hard it is to guffaw without making any noise?

"Hmmm."

"You know that none of this was your fault, don't you, Angie dear? Of course, if you ever remarry, you might try the Saran Wrap idea. There was another suggestion that involved grape jelly, but I can't remember where you spread it exactly. I'll have to pull out the article again and e-mail you. Are you okay, dear?" I had spewed out the pillow with the built-up force of not laughing.

"Yes, fine. Just a tickle in my throat."

"So, now how are the children? And what is new in your life?"

I hope I'm just like Lilah when I grow up. A Southern belle in her mid-eighties, she's as feisty as ever, taking full advantage of her age to do and say the outrageous. She'll lay you out flat with one of her comments, then pick you up and dust you off so charmingly that you forget that she was the one to knock you down in the first place. In her unique way, Lilah had been very supportive ever since Bob left.

"Angie, don't you think it's time you started doing something positive for yourself? You've been quite the drudge lately." *Et tu*, Lilah? "You need to turn the page and start a new chapter, my dear. You can't mope around about the past. You're a relatively young and vital woman. Time to move on. Why, I'd had three husbands by your age. Or was it four?" Lilah had been married at least five times (she thinks there may have been a sixth, one that slipped in during a week in Cuba in 1953, but she's not quite sure). All had ended in divorce, every one of her exes being a "wastrel and womanizer" of some sort. The main difference between my story and Lilah's is that she ended up making sure her "wastrels and womanizers" paid through the nose. Lilah had created a lucrative profit center out of her divorces.

"So what do you intend to do about it, my dear? A nice face-lift always perks me up for a new chapter of life."

"Gosh, I'm not quite sure, Lilah. I guess I'll have to think about it."

"You do that, Angie dear, and let me know what you decide. Tell Tyler and Jenna I love them both dearly and that I'll disinherit them if I don't hear from them soon."

Hanging up, my nagging thoughts ruined any chance of getting back to sleep. Was Lilah right? Were all my best friends right? Was I blocked, unempowered, and a drudge? Maybe I needed to take a good in-depth look at myself, shine the unremitting light of whatever-that-is on my life and see what I discover. To do so, I'd need to a) get out of bed, b) put on a pot of good, strong coffee, and c) find someone who could act as a sounding board. But who? It had to be someone who could be objective, who could be patient, let me come to my own conclusions without a lot of interference. Ah! I had the perfect counselors at my disposal.

"Spud, Alli, get out of bed. I need to talk to you two."

Chapter 5

Talking to my beagles was not a new, weird-old-spinster-living-alone habit I had just adopted. I'd been talking to Spud and Alli for years, finding them infinitely better listeners than my ex-husband. At least the beagles rarely walk out of the room when I'm in midsentence, seldom contradict me in public, and never reveal my most intimate secrets. My most serious discussions are usually with Spud, whom I consider to be the more intelligent of my two beagles because he sits when I say "Sit" and comes when I say "Come." Alli, on the other hand, though generally sympathetic, only pays close attention when certain words come into the discussion: cookie, breakfast, dinner. (Actually, perhaps that indicates that Alli is the more intelligent of the two pups.) For a conversation of this depth and magnitude, I figured I'd need them both. Gathering my beagle advisors by my feet, I sat down with a pad and pen, coffee cup in hand.

"Okay, guys. Either of you know where to start on this?" Spud stood up, scratched at the carpet, and performed the sacred dog ritual of circling his tail three times. He was clearly settling in for a very long session.

I confess that deep introspection had not been a part of my life for years. Who had the time? My thinking focused on the basic survival issues: Should we allow Jenna to dye her hair? (Yes.) Get a tattoo? (No.) Should I stop at the dry cleaners before my meeting or risk that it's closed by the time I head home? (Before the meeting.) Is it too impersonal to address our Christmas cards with computer labels? (Yes, but do it anyway.) I thought about political issues, what to cook for dinner, and how to spruce up the family room. But I didn't do much thinking about "me" per se, who I was, where I was going. Maybe I didn't need to, because for so many years "me" had seemed fairly defined. But now "me" wasn't.

"Let's break it out into categories. What do you think, Spud? Shall we tackle finances first? Can you handle it?" Spud licked his privates, the male beagle version of girding his loins, to consider this thorny subject.

Thanks to good old Marvin, my accountant, I was pretty well up to speed on my financial status. Like a gentle priest explaining death to a child, he had carefully laid the situation out for me.

"Angie, apparently, while Bob's friends were choosing hot red sports cars or cross-country motorcycle trips to express their midlife crises, Bob had chosen speculation in the commodities market."

"Commodities? Like gold and silver futures?"

"Actually, Bob chose to specialize in pork bellies." Of course. How apropos. "He did not choose well. A sports car would have cost forty thousand tops, right? Bob's speculations cost you all of your savings and investments, maxed out your credit cards, and added two additional mortgages on your house. The only thing left untouched is your personal 401(k) which, with the kids in school, you hadn't really started to build yet."

We sat in silence for a few moments while I tried to absorb this. In deference to Marvin, I concentrated on not blacking out, throwing up, or becoming hysterical, all of which struck me as too messy for an accounting office.

I've always thought that the outrageousness of a man's midlife crisis was in direct proportion to the extent his hairline had receded. Bob seemed to support the theory, his few remaining hairs living in different zip codes from one another on his scalp. I looked at Marvin, who was just starting to let a few strands grow long enough to comb across the shiny bald spots. Would he be next? How do mild-mannered accountants express their midlife crises? Maybe they buy really racy-looking calculators or have their social security numbers tattooed across their posteriors. Well, that would be Mrs. Marvin's problem. I had enough of my own.

"So, Marvin, what can I do?"

"Well I've got some ideas, Angie, the most obvious of which is to sell your house and find an inexpensive place to live. Bob should be in position to clear a lot of the debts now." Meaning, of course, the SS *Clarisse*. "And we'll sell whatever is left of the portfolio to clear the rest, though there might be some tax consequences because of the way he set things up." Marvin shook his head and sighed. "You know, Angie, I never did like Bob much."

So dear Marvin helped me through the house sale and

laid out a spending plan going forward, making sure I had a little mad money to spend on extras. After selling the house, I was able to pay off my portion of our debts. Living at Marie's was unbelievably inexpensive, so after all was settled, I found that I could live quite comfortably on my income and even put some money away for a rainy day (though it was hard to imagine that days could get much rainier than they had been the last eighteen months).

"So, Spud, financially we're in pretty good shape right now, and maybe we could even spend a little money on some fun stuff, right?" Spud agreed with a decisive tail wag; Alli was snoring contentedly, having no interest whatsoever in finance.

Next topic? How about career? I don't actually have a career; I have a job, the difference being that I work because I need the money, not owing to any great desire to fulfill myself. My major in college was sociology with a minor in English literature, both equally worthless in the pursuit of livelihood. So for the most part, I had just stumbled into jobs.

When the kids were young, we needed some extra money. So I applied as a part-time office manager for a general contractor/developer.

"Angie, may I call you Angie?" Phil was (and is) the only man I've ever described as courtly. Even in that first interview, his kind, approachable eyes put me instantly at ease. "I want you to understand that I am a man who is starting over. I just lost nearly everything I had in a lawsuit, so I'm building from scratch again. This job may not last if all doesn't go well. I just want to be honest with you."

"Well then, Phil, may I call you Phil? I will be honest with you. I flunked out of typing in high school and I am spastic on an adding machine, but my dad was a CPA, so I have a genetic knack with numbers. I know nothing about construction. But if it has anything to do with getting people to do what they promised to do but what they are not yet doing, I'm a pro because I have two children and a husband. As for scheduling, I am the terror of the pediatric and dental community for my tenacity in getting appointments."

As soon as Phil had stopped laughing, he hired me. I'm still not sure if it was for my qualifications or for comic relief, but it had worked out perfectly for both of us. Phil's business had grown substantially over the years and, because I'm smart and resourceful by nature, I was able to learn all the new skills he needed from me as he expanded and diversified his business. I started out doing basic billing, bookkeeping, and job scheduling. Now, eighteen years later, I was his asset manager, overseeing all of the people, contracts, and services that maintained his large portfolio of properties and investments. I was good at it, enjoyed the diversity, and Phil trusted me implicitly. We kept a small office downtown, though I could just as easily work from home and often did.

For the past three months, Phil had been traveling with his wife Susan, enjoying a well-deserved vacation. I e-mailed reports to him and he called in once a week. Our calls always started with a rundown of whatever exotic place he was visiting at the time: Zanzibar, the Serengeti plain, Kenya. Then we discussed business (Was it time to condominiumize that office complex? Should the roof on that retirement home be replaced now or next winter?) We ended by focusing on me and how I was doing in my new life. Phil, twenty-five years my senior, had always shown a fatherly interest, even more so since the divorce. Our last conversation had been five days before.

"So, Angie, how are you?"

"Well, I'm doing better, Phil. The chaotic part is over. I'm just feeling, well, a little unfocused."

"Of course you are. But you know, Angie, crisis always has some opportunity behind it. You just have to keep your eyes open."

If anyone knew about crisis, it would be Phil. But to look at him now, you would assume his life had been perfect and easy. He was married to a wonderful woman whom he adored. His businesses were to the point where they almost ran themselves, leaving him free to explore the world. He was healthy, vigorous, adventuresome. Maybe there was hope for me.

"I'm sure you're right, Phil. Just a matter of time."

"No, not just time, Angie. You have to be prepared to seize the moment. You have to figure out what you want in life and go out and get it. Know what I mean, Angie?"

For the past eighteen months, "seize the moment" had seemed impossible; seizing my sanity was about all I could handle. But maybe now . . . ?

"Okay, Spud." Spud was the only pup still conscious at that point. Alli, not having heard any of her favorite maybe-food-is-coming words, was still snoozing soundly, reserving her energy for more important matters. "I've got to rate job as Very Satisfactory. It may not last forever with Phil retiring. But we'll tackle that when it happens, okay?"

49

Spud scratched his ear, obviously in perfect agreement with my assessment. Dogs are so reasonable.

Next topic? Health/diet/body. Ugh! Not a fun subject. Every woman in the universe has issues with her body, and I am no exception. When did we get this way? I can't imagine that any of our great-great-grandmothers spent much time worrying about an increase in her cellulite quotient or that her breasts were unlikely to bring in offers from *Playboy*. Women of that time were probably focused on matters like Indian raids or plague or famine. Maybe if we still had to haul water in by the bucket, we'd have less time to consider whether our tummies should be flatter. Maybe those dark little outhouses saved our foremothers from daily examination of their saddlebags and saggy butts, examinations we are forced into by our well-lit bathrooms and full-length mirrors. Maybe the fact that these women only stripped once a month to bathe preserved their physical self-esteem.

Rather than blaming our physical neuroses on those gorgeous supermodel bodies foisted on us by the media, maybe our neurosis started with the advent of indoor plumbing, upgraded hygiene standards, and the eradication of major diseases. Maybe we just need a little pestilence, a bubonic plague epidemic perhaps, to distract us from this obsession with our imperfect bodies. Just a thought.

I am savvy enough to know that no one is interested in the body complaints of a size four. So without droning on, in a nutshell I had become saggy, wrinkly, stiff, and out of shape. My face had become splotchy and sallow-looking from lack of care and exercise, and my neck was looking particularly crepey. Those new pouches under my eyes were testimonials to too many nights crying myself to sleep.

My eating habits? Well, probably not too bad over the last several months if you're willing to consider the five food groups as ice cream (dairy), cookies (grains), wine (fruits and vegetables), and pizza (protein). Is that only four? Well, whatever the fifth food group is, I covered it with chocolate. I had gone from bingeing to simply not eating at all and back to bingeing again. It was a diet only Alli could appreciate. In fact Alli, psychically sensing that the topic was food, had moved into alert status at my feet, ready to assist should the need for a junk-food binge arise.

"I'm sorry, Alli. But we'll simply have to give ourselves a Very Unsatisfactory in the health/diet/body category." Alli put a paw on my thigh in protest. "I understand your concern, but would you buy into it for a doggy cookie?" Her tail wagged ecstatically, as easy to bribe as a French judge at the 2002 Winter Olympics. I gave Alli her doggy cookie and secured her vote.

It was nearly noon, and I decided that my deep introspection needed a break, and my saggy, wrinkly, stinky body needed a shower. Besides, the next topic was intimidating: Relationships/social activities.

As I lathered up, I answered the easy questions. Family? I have wonderful relationships with both of the kids. I have no siblings and, unfortunately, both of my parents had died when the kids were still too young to know them. I have a nice, long-distance bond with a variety of uncles, aunts, and second cousins twice removed, seeing them mainly at weddings and funerals. And my husband, ex-husband? Am I still supposed to carry him on the family roster? When my second cousin Georgia ran off with my cousin Tammy's fiancé, we didn't expel her from the family (though none of us, including Tammy, agreed to be bridesmaids at Georgia's wedding). But I wasn't sure about the etiquette for exes. I'll have to check with Lilah; she should know since she has five (or is it six?) of them.

My friends? Well, my best friends, difficult as they can be, are definitely there for me, though with them I cannot always tell where "there" is. My broader circle of casual friends had virtually disappeared. I had lost touch with the other soccer moms and dads over the years, and my old neighbors had chosen to pledge allegiance to their Neighborhood Watch Captain and her Double Chocolate Cream Cheese Brownies. I can't say I missed these casual friends much, but it did mean that I was spending a lot of time (too much?) by myself, and my social calendar was pretty sparse. I wasn't getting out to do much of anything beyond life-maintenance activities: groceries, gas, work, dry cleaning, etc. My most exotic excursion lately had been to get a mammogram.

And, as my best friends had so rudely observed, my dance card of men friends was totally blank. Was this something that I wanted to change?

I didn't need someone merely for company, like a TV turned on just to have noise in the house. I didn't need someone for "guy duty": getting the oil changed, opening jars, changing ceiling lightbulbs. I had figured out how to get those tasks accomplished by myself, with the added benefit of no guy whining while it was being done. I had also given up the fairy tale of a man taking care of me financially; my experience with Bob obliterated that notion. I was doing fine alone. So what did I want?

I wanted to be loved and cherished. I wanted someone who wanted to hold me when I cry and who would dance with me in the kitchen. I wanted someone who couldn't wait to tell me his news and his worries and his quirkiest thoughts. I wanted someone I could give to, openly, freely, without self-consciousness. I wanted what Marie has with Jack and what Susan has with Phil. What I wanted was rare, but not impossible, was it? Relationships/social activities: another Very Unsatisfactory.

"All right, guys, so we need to work on body/health and the social/relationships. What's our plan?" But Spud and Alli had disappeared, deserting me for an emergency squirrel chase in the backyard. I was on my own. I pulled out a new sheet of paper, wrote Self-Improvement Plan across the top, then crossed it out. Self-improvement was too close to other annoying concepts like diet or budget. I decided to title this plan Angie's New Chapter. Less ominous, more positive and upbeat, don't you think?

Improving my diet and physical condition wasn't going to be so difficult. At least the *planning* to do so wasn't; the doing itself might be another matter. But I'm experienced with the basic requirements. I got myself back into shape after Tyler was born, then again after Jenna. About every five years since then, I'll get disgusted with my body and pull the reins in on myself. Unfortunately, as years progress, the reins require much more strenuous pulling to show any results. The healthy diets had become stricter and lasted longer; the trips to the gym were more frequent and grueling. I hadn't gotten back into shape for at least four years. So I was sure this time I'd have to be on the Dr. Atkins Anti-Everything Diet and find a gym that would let me live on-site.

I wrote down a list of ideas and notes under Body/Health then, as my first step toward a healthier me, cleared out my refrigerator. Of course, I didn't clear out the refrigerator by trashing all of that tasty, healthless food. I just ate my way through it. It was my own little wake, knowing that tomorrow I would be living on wheat grass and tofu.

Tummy full, I sat down and wrote Social/Relationships in big block letters on a brand-new sheet of paper. Okay, a plan, I need a plan. Well, I could, um . . . or maybe, uh . . . what about . . . ? Nope, not one idea, I was stuck. So I borrowed a technique from Winston Churchill, something he used whenever faced with an insoluble problem during the dark days of the war: I took a nap.

Chapter 6

I awoke to a gentle rapping on my door about an hour later. It was Jack delivering my mail.

"Did I catch you at a bad time, Angie?"

"No, Jack, I was just taking a little nap. But I really should get up anyway."

"Why?"

Why, indeed? You have to be careful talking to Jack because he actually listens. Maybe it's his legal training, but he delights in catching people when their mouths keep moving though their minds have disengaged. He leaps on platitudes ("Have a nice day!" : "Compared to what?"), overblown hyperbole("That pie was to die for!" : "You would give your life for a lemon meringue?"), and ill-considered grammar ("Let's do lunch." : "What precisely will we *do* to, for, or with lunch?"). He's not trying to be unkind; his favorite part of the game is to elicit a good comeback.

So I tried, "Um, so I don't wear out my mattress warranty before its time?" Jack laughed.

"You're getting better at this, Angie. So, now that you are up, are you busy with something, or do you have a few minutes?" In Jack's understated way, he was bursting at the seams to show me or tell me about something.

"I've always got time for you, Jack."

"Good, because I just unwrapped my new locomotive. I need someone to come over and admire it, tell me that it is simply extraordinary and absolutely worth the ridiculous amount of money I paid for it."

"I'd be happy to lie to you, Jack. Let me get my shoes."

"Marie has gone hiking, or she could do it. That woman is masterful at making me feel that my dumb decisions are brilliant."

"That's because she honestly believes you to be brilliant." We walked across the forty-five feet from my studio to their house, Spud and Alli at our feet. The pups adore Jack, though I suspect it has something to do with the pouch of dog cookies he has carried ever since we moved in. The model railroad was set up in the basement, which was accessed by one of those slanted doors on the outside that you see in the Midwest.

Though I'd known Jack for ten years, I had only really gotten to know him since I moved into his backyard. His passions are model railroads, jazz, and Marie—not necessarily in that order. Jack viewed the world with a bemused, professorial intellect, which combined with his incessant reading and extensive traveling, made him very entertaining company.

"Well, then Marie's been bewitched by some kind of potion. I just hope she doesn't wake up one day and realize what an old fool she married."

Jack's model railroad setup was not the twelve-foot figure eight loop your brother had as a kid. This installation filled the entire basement and had taken Jack and his train club years to build. Mountains sculpted out of papier-mâché were dotted with tiny perfect evergreens. Serene valleys had deciduous trees, which the club members painstakingly switched out to match each season. Miniature towns, circa 1920, had illuminated windows and streetlamps as well as clock towers that really kept time. The display was a masterpiece, and so massive that I doubt it could ever be relocated. I'm pretty sure Jack will opt to be buried in this house, probably right under the miniature water tower.

I had met people from Jack's train club a few times. There were about twenty members, from all age groups and walks of life: a middle-aged dentist, a retired Marine in his eighties, a high school kid. The one thing they had in common, besides their passion for model trains, was that they were all male. I once heard a woman make the mistake of commenting to Jack that model railroads seemed a silly way for grown men to spend their time.

"Compared to what, madam? There's a hobby group in Great Britain in which the men are fascinated by ancient catapults and how they work. The group researched the original designs and built several of them. Now they have contests catapulting dead cows, pianos, and each other, scoring for distance and style. Compared to that, how silly would you consider us?"

Jack unveiled his new treasure with a flourish. "This, Angie, is a limited edition reproduction of the 2-8-8-2 steam locomotive built in 1919 for the Norfolk and Western Railroad." He continued with the locomotive's history, how it had been used to haul coal in the Appalachians and was then pressed into service to carry troops during WWII. It was actually pretty interesting. When Jack's dissertation seemed to be finished, I took my cue and starting effusing.

"It's incredibly beautiful, Jack. How much did you pay for it? Is that all? Wow! Look at the workmanship, the detail. How ever did you locate such a find?"

Jack beamed. "Thank you, Angie. Very nicely done. That will do. Shall we watch it run now?"

Jack flipped some switches, and the whole display lit up, its trains rolling, its moving parts moving. There is something mesmerizing and soothing about watching model trains run. This is when Jack and I have our best chats.

"So, you and Marie really tied one on last night, huh?" Jack would know this because a) Marie had wisely called him to drive our very inebriated selves home, and b) she always told him absolutely everything. Fortunately, I couldn't quite remember all that had been said the prior night, so I wasn't too embarrassed about any secrets she might have divulged.

"So Marie told you about how she and I first met?" Ooops! I had forgotten that part. Jack fiddled self-consciously with some wires. "I hope she also told you, Angie, that it was the first and last time I ever did something like that."

"Well, no, she didn't, Jack. But it seems to have worked out very well for the two of you, right?"

Jack grinned, the grin of a kid who had known exactly

what he wanted for Christmas and had gotten it. "Absolutely. The methodology was questionable, but the results have been outstanding. So what about you, Angie? How is your life these days?"

"Funny you should ask. I spent all morning thinking about who I want to be when I grow up."

"Growing up is definitely optional." He tooted a couple of his train whistles.

"True. But it's time for me to get on with it and improve certain aspects of my life."

"Sounds like you are ready to leap across the great abyss and begin the next exhilarating phase of your life's journey."

"I guess that's true, Jack." Though "great abyss" sounded a little grand for giving up junk food, and I wasn't sure that new linens would qualify as "exhilarating."

"Well, self-transformation of any kind is invigorating, Angie. And you, like all of us, have so much untapped potential! Did you know that research indicates that involvement in new interests can actually enhance neuropathways in the brain, increasing mental activity by 35 percent or more?" Somehow, I doubted my new regime of stomach crunchies would have this same benefit, but it was possible.

"Angie, my only suggestion, which you are totally welcome to ignore, is to do whatever you have in mind with total enthusiasm. I don't think it's a matter of what you pick exactly. It's that you involve yourself fully in whatever it is. I think that's the key."

And as I watched Jack's pure delight in watching his tiny trains run, I figured he was right.

Chapter 7

Around four-thirty, having tired of introspection, I was clipping my toenails when the phone rang. It was Jenna.

"Mom, let's get together for dinner tonight. There's a new divey little Caribbean place I'd love to introduce you to."

"What? No hot date tonight?" In the cosmic balance of things, Jenna's very active social life more than made up for the vacuum that was mine.

"No, Reggie turned out to be a dweeb."

"Reggie? I thought his name was Steve?"

"Nope, Steve was the dweeb right before Reggie. I'll be by at six, okay?"

"Sounds great, sweetie. What shall I wear?"

A pause. "Mom? You're asking me for fashion advice? Isn't that a little like Barbara Bush asking Queen Latifah for fashion tips?" We both laughed, even though I'm not quite sure who Queen Latifah is.

"Okay, I guess I'll bumble through and figure it out myself. See you soon. Love you, Jenna."

"I love you too, Mom."

Jenna is my free-spirited, highly artistic child. From the time she was a toddler, she insisted on doing things her way, the Jenna way. Her preschool teacher probably captured it best in Jenna's first progress report:

Jenna has an advanced sense of humor and a surprising vocabulary. She is definitely a leader, not a follower, a high-risk taker, though she shows no tendency toward destroying school property at this time. Jenna has a very definite sense of personal style and fashion.

How many preschoolers were noted for their "personal style and fashion"? Jenna started dyeing her hair in rainbow colors by the time she was fifteen. The peacock blue she sported now at twenty-one was my favorite. She wore clothes that would make most of us look like bag ladies, yet were undeniably chic on her.

Jenna speaks her mind with no hesitation but rarely with unkindness. Her friends and boyfriends have been an eclectic group: a concert cellist, a Future Farmer of America, hip-hop performers, high school dropouts and valedictorians. She has a special knack for being able to acknowledge and accept individual faults in people while still appreciating their gifts.

The only really rough time we had as mother and daughter had been in her hormonally driven fifteenth year. That year, Jenna "hated" me, I was "ridiculous" and "a total failure as a mother." I had "never loved" her, "not one little bit." And because of me, her "psyche was irreparably wounded." Fortunately, we made it through that phase without killing each other, and the aliens returned my real daughter to me at the end of the year.

I remember the day Jenna announced her career aspirations. She had just turned seventeen and her pimply face and baby fat had evolved into a beautiful complexion and lithe, graceful body (Dancer? Model?). She was incredibly creative with a flair for the dramatic (An actor? An artist?) and her mind was sharp and insightful (Journalist? Psychotherapist?). But Jenna is never obvious.

"A veterinarian?" I hadn't recalled that Jenna had any particular enthusiasm for the biological sciences. But then again, I could imagine her in a crisp white lab coat, tenderly putting eyedrops in kittens' eyes, delivering puppies, mending wings of tiny birds.

"Yes. Large animals. I think I'll start with livestock, farm animals. But then eventually I'd like to specialize in wild animals."

"Wild animals? Like lions and gorillas and hippopotamuses?"

"Exactly. I could start out in a zoo, then maybe work in one of those reserves in Africa. Doesn't that sound fascinating?"

Well, no, actually, it did not sound fascinating. My 110-pound blue-haired princess wrestling a crocodile to the ground to floss his teeth?

"Jenna, are you really sure this is what you want to do?"

"Of course I'm not sure, Mom! Tyler's the only one in this family who's ever sure about anything. But I do think it's a great idea, it certainly wouldn't lead to a boring, common life, and I'd like to give it a try."

It was always clear that Jenna would never settle for a boring, common (and therefore, safe) life. But a wildlife reserve in Africa? As a consolation, the Universe had provided one of the best veterinary schools in the world just twenty minutes drive from Sacramento, UC Davis. So at least she would be close by for the next few years.

Jenna, eager to get going on her dream, arranged to graduate from high school early ("Won't you miss your prom?" "Mom, why would I want to go to a function where everyone wears scratchy, unnatural clothes that cost way too much only to hear bad music in a stinky old gym, then drive home with a date who has been drinking in the parking lot and throws up all over you?" Put that way, it hardly seemed a loss.) She spent the next four years in preveterinary classes at UC Davis, and had just graduated with honors. Before starting graduate school, she decided to apprentice in a large-animal clinic in a rural area just outside of town.

We got together about once a week for dinner, and I had learned to ask the "how was work" question before we started to eat.

"You shoved your arm up *where?*"

"See, Mom, the calf was in breech position and we had to turn it before it could be born. So I just reached up and . . ."

Jenna picked me up that evening in her VW Beetle, a high school graduation present four years previously. It suited her, cute and funky in fire-engine red, a color that had matched her hair at the time. We drove to the restaurant, and I followed her through the foyer into the dining area.

I always enjoy making an entrance behind Jenna. She is (and I'm not just saying this because I'm her mother—honest!) an absolutely beautiful young woman with her spikey blue hair, perfect complexion, and dark brown eyes. That night, she was wearing a tiny purple T-shirt with a rhinestone pattern on the front, shimmering pencil-thin black pants with boots, and a lacy red shawl thrown over one shoulder. She is a Gen Y knockout, and it's a maternal thrill to watch the faces watching Jenna as she walks by.

"So, Jenna?" We had ordered quickly and were sipping our wine. "In what way did Reggie express his 'dweeb-ness'?"

Dweeb was a pretty broad term in Jenna's vocabulary. One young man had earned the title by being unfaithful, another by driving while under the influence. One of her dweebs had "the IQ of a peanut butter sandwich" and another was "an honest-to-goodness, foaming-at-the-mouth, right-wing fascist."

"Reggie just turned out to be totally boring and full of himself. Every evening, all he wanted to do was sit around watching TV and feeding his face. Kinda like Dad, you know?"

Uh-oh, land mine! I had been extremely careful not to vent about Bob in front of the kids, especially since we had split up. But by the same token, I would have felt very dishonest and hypocritical if I had tried to defend him. My kids were both intelligent and insightful young adults, and I trusted them to come to their own conclusions. I figured my best move was to keep my mouth firmly shut on the matter. And so I did—and I shoved a breadstick in it for extra security.

"You know I love Dad. But I'll never understand what you saw in him."

Chomp, chomp, chomp.

"And that he was stupid enough to choose that lump of lard over you, just for her money, is inconceivable!"

Chomp, swallow, chomp, chomp, chomp,

"Honestly, Mom, Dad was never as smart as you." Chomp, chomp, swallow, chomp. "Never was as interesting or fun to be around as you." Chomp, chomp, chomp, chomp. "And he had really let his body go the past five years. I mean, sex with him couldn't have been great . . ." Chomp, swallow, choke!

"Mom, are you okay?" Jenna had moved around behind me, poised to give Heimlich.

"Yes. No. I'm okay." I sputtered and gasped, slugging down half a glass of wine to dislodge the breadstick logjam in my throat.

"Look, Jenna." My voice was beginning to sound normal again. "You and I have always been very open and honest with each other." Except for the time you snuck out the window to meet up with Jimmy Scott, an adventure you have yet to confess to. "But when it comes to talking about your dad, especially since our divorce, I feel like I'm in an awkward position. He's your dad, and you love him, as you should. I just don't want my grievances with your dad to become your grievances. Know what I mean?"

Jenna looked at me thoughtfully and nodded solemnly.

"Good. So, let's not talk about your dad. But, sweetie, on any other subject, I promise to be totally open and frank with you."

"Really, Mom?"

"Of course. We're entering a new phase of our relationship. More like adult to adult, right?" I took a very adult sip of wine.

"Okay then. How's your sex life?" I spewed my adult sip of wine onto the table and started choking again. I guess I wasn't prepared for how adult our adult-to-adult conversations could get. Jenna thumped me on the back.

"Really, Mom, you've got to start taking smaller sips or littler bites or something."

"Probably right, sweetie." My sputtering subsided again. "All right, I'm okay. Now where were we? Oh, my sex life. Well, let's see. I guess I'd say it was, or is, um, nonexistent."

"Tyler and I figured as much. So how come?"

"You and Tyler have been discussing this?"

"Sure. We've been worried about you, Mom." As polar opposites as Tyler and Jenna seem to be, they have always been extraordinarily close. Maybe it's because Tyler was such a good, protective big brother—and Jenna always seemed to be getting herself into situations from which she needed protection. Or maybe it was because Jenna was constantly there to adore Tyler and make him laugh when life seemed to be overwhelming him. Whatever the reason, I've always cherished this closeness in my kids. Though the thought of the two of them speculating on whether Mom was "getting any" made me cringe more than a little.

"Mom, you don't have to stay alone if you don't want to. You're still very attractive. All my friends say so."

"They do?"

"Uh-huh. Of course, you could spruce yourself up a little."

"I could?"

"Sure, it wouldn't take all that much. And you are very funny and smart."

"I am?"

"Of course, you are. You deserve someone special."

"I do?"

Jenna and I had a very pleasant dinner, her pep talk interspersed throughout the evening. And I marveled once again at the loveliness and wisdom of the young woman sitting across from me.

So when is it exactly that the daughter takes over and starts mothering the mom? I had always figured it would be when I started dribbling down my chin and into my Depends on a regular basis. But I guess it can start sooner. I guess it can start when a mom is feeling as gawky as a thirteen year-old, ready to launch into a new chapter.

When I got home, inspired by Jenna's pep talks and pumped up by my own hours of introspection, I decided to start the Angie's New Chapter campaign by enlisting my three best friends as my mentors in the social/relationships category. I e-mailed each of them the same, very carefully worded question, expressing my full commitment and resolve:

So if I were thinking of maybe attempting to prepare to potentially be open to taking initial steps toward entering arenas where I might someday meet someone, a male someone, and perhaps become romantically involved, though of course only as appropriate, is there some particular aspect of myself that you think I might improve in preparation?

All three of them must have been poised at their computers ready to pounce on such an opening. For by the time I had brushed my teeth, washed my face, and finished getting ready for bed, I had responses from all three. Their replies could be distilled as the following:

Gwen: Knowledge
Jessica: Ambience
Marie: Underwear

Chapter 8

Getting up Sunday morning, I decided to start with Underwear as the more definitive and probably more achievable recommendation.

"So Marie." She and Jack had just returned home from church. She brought me a latte, a chai for herself, and muffins to share, a Sunday morning ritual we had started when I had moved in.

"Don't you think leaping into the underwear stage is a little premature? I mean, aren't there a few stages in between 'Angie doesn't even know any eligible men' and 'Angie exposes her panties.'"

"Hmmm." Marie took several slow, considered sips of her chai before continuing. "You know, Angie, lingerie is not really about what others see, though at some point, of course, we would want that to become a consideration. It's more about how you feel. And when you feel a certain way about yourself, you exude a particular energy, a magnetism. And it's that energy that attracts men to you."

I chewed on this thought and my cranberry muffin for a moment. If anyone knew about the exuding and attracting thing, it would certainly be Marie.

"So what 'certain way' am I supposed to feel? And how would underpants and a bra get me there? Are we talking metal-studded bustiers and leather garter belts?"

"Angie, you are too funny!" Really? I wasn't trying to be. "Come on. Put your shoes on. We're going on a field trip." An underwear field trip? I remembered all of those field trips when the kids were little. Should I pack a lunch? Get a permission slip from someone who was more adult than I was?

As we drove to the mall, Marie talked about something or other that I completely missed. My mind was too absorbed in anxious images of edible thongs, crotchless bikinis, plunging backless, strapless bras (How the heck did those things stay up anyway? Were they surgically attached?).

Marie marched me into a pink, frilly, and highly scented Victoria's Secret. I had never been inside one before and felt totally intimidated. My underwear purchases typically came in plastic three-packs from JC Penney. At Penney's, you find underwear tucked discreetly between the dish towels and the luggage. I grew up in a household where undergarments are supposed to stay *under* something. But Victoria's Secret is an entire store devoted to nothing but underwear and all the stuff that is supposed to remain unseen exposes itself in full public view. Where's the secret in *that*?

"Okay, Angie, I'm going to check in the back and see if my special order came in. Why don't you just browse around and get some ideas. Then we'll start trying things on."

Trying things on? It's one thing for those perfectly shaped bodies to wear this stuff, but me? With my wrinkly, saggy little butt and boobs? Okay, deep breath. I can do this, I'm an adult. And I'm entering my new chapter.

I moved slowly, self-consciously through the store with its lacy displays and racks of satiny fabrics, avoiding eye contact with the other shoppers. Surely I was being pegged as the desperate middle-aged single woman on the prowl, and I prayed none of my old neighbors would happen by. *Hey, I saw old Angie Hawkins the other day, dumped by her husband and driven to sleazy underwear.*

But as I walked around I realized that the garments on the racks weren't sleazy at all. Most of them were pretty, though some were a little extreme for me. But then again, I lived in the world of three-to-a-package cotton briefs.

I also began to notice that the other shoppers looked, well, normal. Not desperate or perverted or kinky at all. Most of the shoppers were women, but there were a few brave male shoppers asking earnest questions of the professional-looking salesclerks. The other women shoppers were of all ages, body types, marital statuses. Everyone was walking around unself-consciously, inspecting garments that my mother would have warned me against if she had known they existed. Apparently, there had been a whole cultural revolution that I had missed, a fancy-underwear revolution. Where had I been?

"There you are." Marie had a large pink bundle, and I was dying to know what she had special ordered. But, being new to the world of lingerie, I wasn't sure it was good etiquette to ask. "Did you see anything you like, Angie?"

"Well, um, yes, sort of. But, Marie, I have no idea where to start! It's all so overwhelming."

"Hmmm." Marie gave me one of her long, penetrating Marie looks. "Okay. Then let's get you started with a Miracle Bra." A Miracle Bra? Some kind of antigravity device? "So, what size are you?" She led me toward the back of the store.

"Thirty-four B. Well, actually, I'm more like a wannabe 34 B but the 34 A's are usually too tight."

"Got it. No problem." Marie shuffled through some racks and drawers until she had a colorful stack of bras for me to try on.

"So Angie, what's your panty size?"

"Um, 5? 6? I never remember."

Marie looked at me quizzically. A grown woman who doesn't know her own panty size? The underpants I usually bought were in color-coded packages. I don't think they had numbers; I was size yellow. She led me over to a table covered with neat piles of little smidgens of lace, satin, and silk. I picked one smidgen up.

"A pair of thongs? Oh, no, Marie. I couldn't! They are just too . . . I would be too, uh . . . ."

"Angie, it's called a 'thong,' not a 'pair of thongs.' " 'Thongs' are those flip-flop things you wear at the beach."

"Oh. A thong then. But my rear end would just feel too . . . it wouldn't cover my, uh . . . ."

Marie ignored my stammering and pawed through the piles. "It's all in the fit, Angie. See, you pick a size larger than your normal panty size, then test that the length of the waistband to the crotch is longer than the span of your thumb to your pinky, hand full spread." She spread my fingers and laid them on a velvet thong. "See? These would be just right, perfectly comfortable." I remained skeptical as Marie shoved the bundle of tiny thongs (If *thongs* means sandals, what is the plural of *thong?* Is it like fungus/fungi? Thongi?) into my hands and steered me toward the dressing room.

"Now go get started with this, and I'll grab some other stuff."

Another deep breath. I stripped off my trusty old cotton bra, which was beginning to look pretty homely next to its more elegant cousins. I picked up one of the fancy bras, which turned out to be an underwire contraption with some kind of liquid filling in the lower third of each cup. How odd. Wonder if this leaks? Would it freeze up in winter? I put it on and—Va Voom! My nondescript little bust was instantly transformed! It stood out, round and proud and I had—oh my gosh!—cleavage! Now THAT was a miracle!

Marie found me laughing out loud when she returned, her arms laden with more goodies to try on.

"Marie, look at me! I'm positively stacked." She smiled, though I could see that the true thrill of the moment was lost on her, coming as she was from her 36D perspective. I spent the next hour and a half trying on everything from the sublime (a teddy studded with semiprecious stones) to the mundane (though the Victoria's Secret version of mundane still put my old cotton undies to shame). Marie made several forays back to the sales floor until our dressing room was packed.

At one point, Marie ducked back into the dressing room, whispering, "Guess who is out there?"

"Who?"

"The one and only Clarisse, Home Wrecker Extraordinaire."

"You're kidding. Really?"

We poked our noses out of the dressing room to get a peek. I hadn't seen Clarisse since I had sold the house, she having had the nerve to show up to my garage sale. I did NOT give her a bargain on the Christmas napkins she purchased.

She looked pretty much the same, and she chatted with the cashier as if they were old friends. The clerk folded several colorful, silky items into Clarisse's pink-striped bag. Marie and I looked at each other, reminding ourselves silently how unkind it was to make snide remarks about extremely overweight women. Especially overweight women who were incredibly wealthy widows. Wealthy widows who stole other people's husbands. And probably did so wearing Victoria's Secret lingerie. Marie cracked first.

"I'm picturing a Sumo wrestler, heavyweight division, wearing a purple velvet bustier with matching string bikini."

We guffawed heartily before my guilty conscience caught up to me. "We shouldn't, Marie. It's not very nice."

"Why? Because she's fat? She's a husband stealer, Angie. That makes any requirement for being politically correct null and void. I would have made fun of a skinny husband stealer as well."

"Oh, really? What would you have said?"

Marie's answer was almost instantaneous. "How about, 'That woman would have to wear a Miracle Bra just to qualify as flat-chested.' Or, 'When God created that woman's buns, he must have used the unleavened bread recipe.' "

We cracked up again. Who knew buying undies could be so much fun? Actually, who knew that Marie could be so fun? It must have been her protectiveness of me that brought out the Don Rickles side of her. When we caught our breaths, we peeked out to see Clarisse exiting with her bundle.

"Looks like she comes here all the time. Marie, even Clarisse wears fancy lingerie!" Though the image of her in it was not particularly attractive. "Am I the only woman in the universe who is still wearing cotton briefs and eighteen-hour bras?"

Marie looked at me with complete seriousness. "Yes, Angie. You are."

Fortunately, Marie has extensive product knowledge when it comes to intimate apparel. Our dressing room was jammed with lingerie, and I really needed help deciding what to buy.

"Those are good because they won't show a panty line even in your tightest slinky dress." (I don't actually own a tight slinky dress, but I figured it was good to be prepared.). "Nope, not that. It will be too difficult to take off at the critical moment." (I wasn't clear whether the critical moment had to do with a lustful urgency or the need to pee, but agreed that I shouldn't risk it.) I ended up with several combinations for everyday wear, a couple of special occasions sets, and one set for "the moment of truth."

Loaded down with our big pink parcels, we stopped at an ice-cream shop in the mall. Unlike most of my friends, Marie never seems to worry about what she eats, often quoting Erma Bombeck: "Remember all of those ladies on the *Titanic* who waved off the dessert cart!" She ordered her ice-cream sundae with extra chocolate sauce and absolutely no guilt. And because I was with Marie, I did the same.

"So now we need to find you some sleepwear. What do you sleep in now?"

"Oh, just some great big old T-shirts." I was enjoying my sundae, wondering how Marie persuaded her ice cream to transform itself into luscious curves on her body rather than as mine did, to little lumps on my saddlebags.

"Hmmm. T-shirts?" Uh-oh. She was giving me one of those Marie looks but I couldn't see where she was going with it. "And where exactly did you get those great big old T-shirts?"

"Oh, I don't know, Marie, I've had them for a million years. I suppose originally they belonged to . . .um, Bob." I cringed. How could I be so completely oblivious? I had been officially divorced for a whole twelve months and separated for six months before that. Yet here I was still wearing my ex-husband's old T-shirts to bed every single night! And they were *ugly* T-shirts of sports teams I didn't like and car products I didn't understand.

We shared a very long silence while I (we) contemplated my utter obtuseness once again.

"Angie, let me ask you something. Is it that you want Bob back?" I looked up into Marie's intense hypnotic eyes. She was like one of those snake charmers, and I could feel that she was about to draw answers out of me that I didn't know I had.

"No, that's not it. I mean, I wouldn't have ended the marriage myself. When we married, it's like Bob became family. And you don't just desert family because they get boring or overweight or even because they create financial disasters for you. And so I wouldn't have chosen to leave Bob." As I spoke these words, I knew they were true. Marie's snake-charmer eyes kept drawing me out.

"And yet after he left? Honestly, I felt relieved, Marie. It's hard to admit it, it makes me feel so disloyal, but I was truly relieved, like a weight had been lifted."

"So what about the lifestyle you had to give up, Angie? Being married, the house . . ."

I thought for a moment, letting Marie's hypnotic eyes lead me to the truth. "Well, no, I guess I don't really miss any of that either. At first, it hurt to leave the house and all of its memories. But I think I would have just suffocated myself in those memories. So I'm not sorry now that the house is gone."

"But you're missing something, Angie. What do you suppose it is?"

"If there's anything that I'd like back, I guess it's the certainty."

"The certainty?"

"Yes. The certainty of knowing who I am and where exactly I fit in. Only I don't want to be the 'who I am' that I was, and I don't want to fit in where I fit before, but someplace new."

"Ah. I see." And I could tell that Marie really did see.

"So, Angie, even though you have pretty much let go of the past, you're not really sure about the future. And that's probably a little scary, huh?"

My lower lip started to quiver. "Yes, scary."

"And maybe a little lonely?"

"Yes. Lonely." The inevitable tears started streaming. So much for my mascara.

"So, you know what I think, Angie?"

"What?" I took the tissue Marie offered and started dabbing at the black streaks down my cheeks.

"I think it's time for you to take a very bold step and buy some new pajamas. And when we get home, we'll have a ceremony ripping up Bob's old T-shirts into shreds. They will make excellent dust cloths!"

Our next stop was the lingerie department at Nordstrom, and I quickly learned that Marie has very definite rules about sleepwear.

"No flannel, no plaids. No grandmother collars, no cutesy animal patterns. Colors must be pretty and soothing and, in your case Angie, less likely to show dog hairs."

She also led me away from the diaphanous negligees, fearing that a transition from T-shirts to negligees might be too big a shock on my system. So we ended up with an assortment of soft, cozy silk and satin pjs and nightshirts. We also found a lovely, warm bathrobe and some angora bed socks to use "just until you find yourself a living, breathing foot warmer."

We headed home with a trunkload of my beautiful new intimates and my slightly shell-shocked credit card. I wonder if this is what Marvin, my accountant, had meant by "spend a little something on yourself." I'd have to ask him. I crossed Underwear off the Angie's New Chapter list.

Chapter 9

It took a few days of voice mails back and forth to catch Gwen.

"So what exactly do you mean by Knowledge? I do know where babies come from, Gwen."

I swear I could hear Gwen rolling her eyes to the ceiling. "Angie, there is a lot more to the male/female dynamic than the mechanics of reproduction. Meet me at Barnes & Noble after work, say six o'clock?"

Oh, goody! It looked as if most of Angie's New Chapter was going to be launched via shopping. I could handle that.

When I arrived at the bookstore, Gwen, list in hand, was already at the Information counter talking to a lanky, pimply young man with miscellaneous tattoos, a ring in his eyebrow, a stud in his tongue, wearing a Grateful Dead T-shirt from a concert that took place long before he was born.

"Oh, good! Here she is. This is my friend who is looking for all of these books." Gwen handed Mr. Information the list. He looked at the list, looked at me, looked at the list again, and shrugged.

"Hey, cool, whatever. Just, like, follow me to the Sexuality and Sexual Dysfunction section."

I remember reading once that when you blush your entire body actually blushes, not just your cheeks. At that particular moment, I was certain this theory was true. Either that, or I was having the Mother of All Hot Flashes.

"Well, er, um, maybe you could just point us in the general direction and . . ."

"No, no, no, Angie. It's this young man's job to assist us. Did you say your name is Kevin? I'm sure you are really good at finding books, right, Kevin? We're keeping this young man gainfully employed by making use of his professional services, aren't we, Kevin?"

Oh, well, gosh, of course. We wouldn't want to jeopardize Kevin's job security just to preserve my last little shred of dignity. The three of us headed merrily off to find the Sexuality and Sexual Dysfunction section.

We came to the aforementioned aisle (did you even know they had such a section?) and Kevin checked Gwen's list. "Let's see. *The Big O, Orgasms: How to Have Them, Give Them and Keep Them Coming.* Okay, *The Big O, The Big O* . . . Ah-ha! Here it is! *The Big O, Orgasms: How to Have Them, Give Them and Keep Them Coming!*" Kevin's booming voice clearly indicated his pride in finding the book so quickly. I guess the convention of speaking in hushed tones in libraries does not carry over to bookstores. Pity. Kevin handed me the book with a flourish. Don't these things come in plain brown paper wrappers? I tried to smile my appreciation, but I think my facial muscles had frozen into an expression of pre-guillotine horror. The resulting grimace could not have been pretty.

However, Kevin was on a roll by then and his enthusiasm could not be dampened. "Okay, one down and fourteen to go! Next? Um, *How to Drive your Man Wild in Bed.* Okay, *Drive Your Man Wild, Drive Your Man Wild . . .*"

During the next eon (okay, maybe four minutes) that we spent in the Sexuality and Sexual Dysfunction section, Gwen browsed with her normal intellectual curiosity. "Oh. Look, Angie. *A Complete Guide to Sado-Masochism.* How interesting." See, to Gwen, a book is just a book. And knowledge of any sort is . . .

". . . power, Angie. Knowledge is power." Gwen and I were sitting in the coffee bar after our extensive bookstore tour with Kevin, perusing my stash of new books. Only five of the books had come from the Sexuality and Sexual Dysfunction section. We had also visited the Self-Help section:

"Here we go! *Smart Women, Dumb Choices.*"

"Thank you, Kevin." I had chosen to take that title as a compliment. Then the Health and Beauty section:

"I found it! *MakeUp for Dummies.*" So I took the compliment back from myself. Gender Issues:

"*Men Are from Mars.* Gosh, this is an oldie. Didn't know it was still in print. Oh, and here's *The Stronger Sex: Understanding and Resolving the Eternal Power Struggles Between Men and Women.* This one weighs a ton!" I slipped the ton of gender power struggle resolving back on the shelf, hoping Gwen wouldn't notice. And finally, the Divorce Issues section:

"*Dumped: A Survival Guide for the Woman Who's Been Left by the Man She Loved.* So who got dumped?"

"That would be me, Kevin."

By the time we had located all of the books on Gwen's list, and Kevin, Gwen, and I had engaged in a spirited debate over the merits of various versions of the Kama Sutra (Photographs or illustrations? Original text or modern interpretation?), most of my embarrassment had dissipated, or at least gone into remission for the time being. So at coffee afterward, I was ready to discuss our choices out loud.

"But, Gwen, do you really think I need to know how to 'drive any man wild in bed' before I've even met a potential candidate?"

"Angie, I don't expect you to be doing anything specific with the information right away. It's just that studying about sex and learning to be more proficient in bed will make you a little more confident in yourself. And when you feel more confident in yourself . . ."

". . . I'll exude a certain energy that will be attractive to men."

"Precisely. And some of those other books will help fill in some of your general lack of experience with men, give you some sense of how they think, what they need from a woman, etc., etc."

"What do you mean my 'general lack of experience with men'? I was married for over twenty-six years!"

"Angie, you were married to a troglodyte." Did I mention that none of my friends had ever liked Bob? "I'm talking about real men, Angie. Men who are smart and romantic and loyal and caring. Like Wayne."

Wayne is Gwen's longtime, long-distance boyfriend. He lives in San Francisco, about two hours away. The two of them spend every other weekend together and head off on vacations three or four times per year. I'd only met him a few times. He seemed nice enough and certainly a match for Gwen in intellect.

"So why have you and Wayne never married?"

Gwen smiled. "Because it works so well this way, Angie. We both cherish our freedom. We avoid the mundane 'which toothpaste do we buy' compromises that being married would require, and our times together are always special events. This kind of thing may not work for everyone but I can relate to a quote I heard from Katharine Hepburn. She wasn't much for marriage but preferred her man 'to live close by and visit often.' It works for me."

Interesting idea. I guess in my vague thinking about such things I had seen only two options: lonely singlehood or marriage. I had never thought of anything in between.

"One of the benefits of this kind of arrangement, Angie, is that it is less likely that the woman in the couple loses herself within the relationship, which is so very common."

"What do you mean 'loses herself'? Like the toothpaste compromise?"

"No, I mean loses a sense of herself, who she is, what she likes, and what she wants out of life. Like you did within your marriage."

"I did not 'lose' myself!"

"Yes, you did."

"No, I didn't. I still know what I like."

"Really? Then tell me, Angie, what is your favorite type of cheese?"

"Colby Jack."

"I see. And why is that your favorite type of cheese?"

"Because, um, it's good." And because that's the only

kind of cheese Bob would eat. He said it melted best on toasted cheese sandwiches.

"Interesting. If I recall, when we were in college, you had a thing for Brie and warm French bread."

She had me. She knew it, and I knew it. Unfortunately, Gwen is not diplomatic enough to just let our communal knowings remain unspoken.

"So, Angie, you've got to admit that you have totally lost yourself. You don't know what movies you like or what your mission in life is. You can't remember what your dreams for yourself were or how you really like to spend a Sunday afternoon. Honestly, I think you are extremely lucky that Bob dumped you so you can find yourself again."

I'm not sure "extremely lucky" is how I would have described it, but I wasn't about to challenge Gwen when she was on a roll. She did have a point, and I'd have to digest it later. But I wasn't in the mood for another feminist diatribe, so I feinted and changed the subject.

"Oh, Gwen, I almost forgot to mention that Tyler is coming back into town to interview for a position with an old classmate of yours, Judge Bennett. Apparently, an unexpected opening."

"Beatrice the Bitch? Oh, my gosh, poor kid! I'm not surprised there's an opening. They probably have to give her staff hazard pay."

"What do you mean?"

"Angie, that woman is one of the most petty, jealous, vindictive human beings to walk the earth. I remember once she had a boyfriend in law school who outscored her on an exam. She broke up with him immediately and, though they never proved that she was the one who did it, framed him in a cheating scandal that got him kicked out of school. I run into her occasionally now. She seems to have gotten even worse as she's aged."

"Oh, my gosh! We need to warn Tyler!"

"Angie, the legal profession is rough, and he'll be running into sharks sooner or later."

"Well, it would be nice if he didn't lose a limb to one of those sharks on his very first real job! Are we just supposed to stand by and watch him get slaughtered by some Harvard bitch with obvious pathological inclinations? Of all people, Gwen, how in good conscience could you remain silent and allow a sincere young person like Tyler to get annihilated, as if it's some kind of hazing for new attorneys?" Do you think that maybe I get overly dramatic when my children are threatened? No, I don't either.

"Okay, Angie, calm down! Perhaps you're right." My ferocious mommyness must have frightened her because Gwen rarely backs down so easily. "Let me think about it. I'll talk to Tyler and give him some pointers."

"I expect no less from you, Gwen."

"But you know what I'll never understand about you, Angie?"

"What?" I kept my voice huffy to remind her that Mother Bear was still on alert.

"You can be absolutely relentless where your children are concerned, frightening really. And you've got the reputation of being a pretty tough businesswoman, especially since that Verducci incident."

That Verducci incident had to do with a subcontractor that I, with Phil's blessing, sued for fraud. We ended up in arbitration, a process that left the blustering Mr. Verducci $175,000 poorer. The man is six-five but still scurries into hiding whenever he sees me coming.

"So?"

"So how is it that you can be such a tough cookie in other areas and yet such a total wimp in your own personal life?"

Good question.

Chapter 10

I wasn't able to reach Jessica until the end of the week. Her job as a facilitator/project planner for large corporations often has her on the road. But she returned my call as soon as she got back into town that Friday.

"So, Jessica, what do I need to do about Ambience?"

I was roaring full blast into my New Chapter. I had replaced all of my old underwear with my new purchases and had even dared to wear a "special occasion" set to work on Thursday. It did make me feel, well, different somehow, almost sexy.

I had delved into several of Gwen's books. The Lou Paget books (*The Big O* and *How to Be a Great Lover*) were fun and easy to read. The whole idea of studying to be a proficient sex partner was starting to seem quite normal. So how come I never knew you could take lessons and become skilled at sex? I always assumed that sex was something that you're either good at or not, and honestly, I didn't know which group I fell into. Has every woman in America but me read these books? Well, maybe not.

Maybe just all the women in Massachusetts, the state with the lowest divorce rate in the country. Maybe the books aren't even available in Arkansas and Nevada, where divorces are as common as head colds.

So I was ready to tackle Ambience. "No, problem, Angie. How about if we meet at your place at five?"

I greeted Jessica with a cup of Lively Lemon tea at the door when she arrived, and announced, "You know, Jess, it's not that I need to improve the ambience of this place specifically so I can entertain someone. It's just that it will help give me a certain sense of myself, an energy that will be attractive to men, magnetic you might say." I may not be much, but I am definitely trainable.

Jessica looked surprised. "You're absolutely right, Angie. In fact, I think your heart chakra is looking more open already." I'm pretty sure what she saw was the effect of my Miracle Bra, but I didn't correct her.

"Okay," she said, rubbing her hands together. "Where shall we begin? Give me a few moments, Angie. I need to check the Feng Shui of your place and the layout of your furniture."

I stood to the side and watched Jessica go to work. She sat in every chair, turning each one to face every direction possible. She flopped down on the bed, first with her head on the pillow, then with her feet on the pillow, then across it sideways. She opened up cupboards and looked in the refrigerator.

"Angie, I'm famished. Would you have a bit of cheese?"

Jessica walked through the front door frontward and came back through backward. She sat down on the toilet (seat down), then turned and stood facing it (seat up). She pulled open drawers and scrutinized my framed family photos. Finding one that included Bob, she turned it face-down with a significant look in my direction. I started getting a little anxious when she kicked off her shoes, hopped on the bed, and started jumping up and down.

"Jess, what on earth are you doing?" Spud and Alli leaped up and joined her, barking their approval of this new game.

"Oh, nothing really. I just think every bed deserves a few good bounces before it's put out to pasture." She got down, slightly breathless, and rebuckled her Mary Janes. "So, there's good news, and there's bad news."

"Should I sit down for this?"

"Sure, if you want, but turn your chair to the East. First the good news: the basic Feng Shui of your place is very good. So we won't have to reposition the bathroom or the front door or anything."

Oh, my, that was very good news! Kind of like going in to get the windshield washer fluid in your car topped off and the mechanic announces, "Hey, good news! We won't have to rebuild your engine!" I took a gulp of Lively Lemon. "And the bad news?"

"Well, that bed absolutely must go. And you definitely need new linens, pillows, candles, and probably some silk flowers."

I brightened. "So we're going shopping?"

"Yep, we're going shopping."

Yes! This was the part of self-improvement that my self really liked.

Our first stop had to be for the least fun, most expensive item, the bed. Having not bought a new bed in more than twenty years, I felt a little overwhelmed entering Mattresses Galore. But Jessica marched us in confidently, as nonchalant as if we were buying a quart of milk.

"First, we need to find just the right salesperson." She scrutinized the candidates critically. "Him. That one over there." She headed toward a fairly attractive man standing in one corner of the store. He looked to be about forty, six feet tall with a nice ready-to-serve-you smile in place. I couldn't see anything particularly different about him; maybe his mattress chakra was glowing.

Jessica cornered him, squinted at his name tag, and reached out to shake his hand. "Hello, uh, Russ. I'm Jessica, and this is my friend, Angie. We are looking for a bed for Angie, queen size. And though Angie is single, we don't expect her always to be alone in her new bed, if you know what I mean. We picked you because you are probably about the right height and body type of the kind of guy she finds attractive, and therefore the type who might be in bed with her in the future. So we thought you might be able to help her test out different mattresses."

Russ was momentarily stunned but recovered quickly. I suppose when you sell mattresses for a living, you hear some pretty interesting stories. Stories that the guy in the shoe department probably never hears. Russ looked at me and smiled. "Well, now, I must tell you up front that I am a happily married man."

"Oh, no, Russ. We're only asking you to lie on the mattresses with her, to give her a sense of how it feels with someone else in bed with her." And with that, Jessica hooked her arm through his and headed off to the queen section across the store.

91

As for me? I couldn't move. You know that phrase "die of embarrassment"? Well, there may actually be some medical basis for it, because at that moment, my entire body ceased to function. I was frozen to the spot, and I'm sure I had stopped breathing completely.

While standing there in my complete paralysis, I contemplated the whole issue of embarrassment and its place in my life experience. In truth, until a week ago, I would have to say that it really had not been one of the main themes in my life. But starting with my birthday, announcing my sorry celibacy in public, trotting around fancy underwear stores, rummaging through X-rated bookstore aisles—well, embarrassment was becoming a constant companion. Was I handling it better? Oh, I think so. But it's just that there were always new surprises. Like when your friend sets you up with a complete stranger to act as a surrogate bed partner to test out mattresses at Mattresses Galore. Should I have foreseen this? Was I lacking in imagination?

"Angie!" Jessica's voice, as soothing as squealing brakes coming up behind you at a red light, broke my reverie. "Come on! Russ has found some beds that he thinks you two will really enjoy together!"

I spent the next forty-five minutes bouncing around on beds with Russ while Jessica yelled out instructions like a militant square dance caller.

"No, no! Don't sit your way into the bed. Always flop in. Good. Now Angie, you squirm around while Russ stays still. Fine. Now Russ, you toss and turn while Angie stays still. Okay. Now both of you, spoon to the left. Good. Now spoon to the right. Fine. Okay so how was that one?"

By the fourth bed, both Russ and I loosened up and got into the swing of things. We tried to flip our spoons with military precision, more often than not clunking heads in the process. We developed our own "cold shoulder" position, lying on opposite sides of the bed as far apart as possible without falling off. Periodically, one of us would say, "It was good for me. Was it good for you?" and we giggled uncontrollably. Jessica had to get a little stern at times to keep us on the task at hand. But, finally, we found a mattress that both Russ, representing all those within the male species who might one day have the privilege of entering this bed, and I agreed upon.

I paid up and arranged for the mattress to be delivered the next evening. "And will you be requiring a delivery person of a certain height and body type as well?" Russ grinned.

"Shut up, Russ." One of the shortest routes to breaking through barriers between strangers is apparently to bounce around on beds together. "Go home and tell your wife all about your evening at work." I wanted to add that this was the most fun I'd had in bed with a man for years, but I thought it sounded a little too pathetic.

Next stop, the linens store.

"Okay, Angie, we're looking for sheets that are smooth and sensuous."

"Smooth and sensuous."

"Yes. And you want to test them with the inside of your wrist or your cheek. Someplace sensitive. And don't rely on laundering to soften sheets up. If they start out scratchy, they'll always be scratchy. So you need a high thread count."

93

"Okay. High thread count. Uh, what about satin sheets?"

"Angie, I really wouldn't recommend those for a novice. They tend to slip and slide, and you'll find yourself squished out onto the floor like a pickle from a gooey sandwich."

Hmmm. Not a romantic image. "Okay. But what about colors? Should they be red or black or something?" I didn't really like those colors but figured they were supposed to represent passion.

"Good grief, no! Those would be all wrong for you energetically. Let's go for peaches or pinks, aquas, greens. Think soft and feminine."

"Soft and feminine. Right."

As we worked our way through the store, I soon discovered that "smooth and sensuous, soft and feminine" also translated into incredibly expensive.

"Jess, I have never spent this much on a sheet in my entire life!"

"But Angie, look at your track record in the bedroom in your life thus far. Not much to rave about, right?"

"You think that was all due to cheap, scratchy sheets?"

"Of course not. Well, at least not entirely. But Angie, think of it this way. You will spend at least a third of your entire life in bed in those sheets either sleeping or doing something more amusing. A third of your life! Shouldn't you make sure you feel wonderful there?"

Well, put that way, it made perfect sense to spend half a month's salary on bed linens.

"So now we need pillows."

"But, Jess, I've got a pillow."

"Not pillow. Pillows, plural. A mountain of throw pillows on your bed expresses comfort, luxury, the Universal Womb."

"Is the Universal Womb sexy?"

"Nothing sexier."

"Okay, so throw pillows. How many is a mountain?"

Did I say the mattress store would be our most expensive stop? It wasn't. By the time we left the linens place, I had two sets of sheets, a comforter, duvet, frilly pillow shams and a matching bed skirt, sixteen throw pillows, sachets for the linen closet, and lavender water to sprinkle on the aforementioned sheets. My credit card gave a little whimper as I returned it to my wallet, and we decided to postpone candles and flowers for another excursion. I firmly crossed Ambience off my checklist.

Chapter 11

Over the next couple of weeks, I settled into enjoying the new purchases for my New Chapter. I read more in the books, skipping around from lessons on the intricacies of personal lubricants to writing exercises designed to help me figure out my soul's true mission. I experimented with combinations of my new undergarments and wore different pretty pajamas to bed every night, nuzzled in my fragrant, soft new sheets.

And I thoroughly enjoyed my mountain of throw pillows. Jessica was right; they formed a womblike atmosphere on the bed. The pups and I loved burrowing into them, playing hide-and-seek, nuzzling within the pillow mountain for cozy naps. We left the pillows on the bed while we slept at night. It reminded me of when, as a little girl, I had slept with a crowd of dolls and stuffed animals in the bed with me. The least-favored toys, of course, were packed into the outside edges of the bed, where they might inadvertently be pushed out onto the floor, the price to be paid for being naughty.

My best friends called in frequently to check on me, each having adopted my New Chapter as her own special project.

"So, Angie, I saw this slinky little knit that I think would be perfect for you. It's on sale in a shop on J Street . . ."

"Angie, did you see the Learning Exchange catalogue? There's a class called Dating the Second Time Around that you should consider attending . . ."

"Angie, there is a sale on scented candles at the mall. Ylang-ylang is romantic or maybe citrus. Avoid citronella, unless you've got mosquitoes . . ."

With all of these suggestions and the exercises and recommendations from my books, I found myself quite busy. I headed off on a new expedition just about every night, like the night I went on the Great Condom Mission.

In one of Lou Paget's books, I had read that *a self-confident woman who values herself will always provide supplies to ensure her safety.* I'm not sure my self-confidence was really up to par, but I figured I'd better get the supplies in anyway. So one night after work, I decided to go for it.

I didn't want to go to my old pharmacy, the place where I had ordered Pedialyte, Baby Tylenol, Bob's Rogaine, and my estrogen pills. I had not yet been to the pharmacy near Marie's but was hesitant to make this my first introduction to the place. *Hey, here comes the condom lady!* So I drove a few miles out of my way after work one night and stopped at a Walgreen's.

I'd never actually purchased condoms before. When I was married to Bob, the responsibility for contraception was assumed to be mine. (I can just hear Gwen's voice:

"Troglodyte!"). So I'd been through decades of birth control pills, IUDs, and diaphragms. But I remembered seeing condoms tucked discreetly near the pharmacy window.

Not quite ready to plunge into the condoms, I reconnoitered my way slowly through the store. I hit the greeting card aisle and found cards for all birthdays and occasions three years forward. I bought myself a fistful of travel-sized odds and ends, just in case I needed to head off on some spontaneous, wild weekend. And I picked up a two-year supply of dental floss. Having filled my basket with a dozen things I didn't want or need, I decided it was time to brave the contraceptives aisle.

Wow! I was stunned. Four whole shelves of Trojans, LifeStyles, MAXX, PleasurePlus. Where to begin?

"May I help you?" I jumped. A very efficient-looking young woman in a white pharmacist's jacket had appeared at my elbow.

"Uh, well, yes, of course. I'm, er, probably looking for some condoms."

"Probably?"

"No, I mean, certainly. I am certainly looking for some condoms. Nonlatex, please." I had read in my *Big O* book that latex can cause all sorts of sores and infections, and I was proud of my sophisticated knowledge.

"Of course. And in what size?"

"Size?"

"Yes. What size condom?"

"Oh, what size condom. Well, I guess I'm not really sure."

"Well, what size is he?"

"He who?"

"Him." She pointed to a virile-looking young man on a Trojan box who was holding a very happy-looking woman.

"Him? Oh, you don't mean *that* him. You mean *my* him."

"Yes." This young pharmacist was very patient, seeming completely comfortable discussing condoms with a blithering, stammering middle-aged nincompoop. I'll bet she dealt with a lot of dementia patients.

"Well, let's see. He's about, um . . ." How big are those things anyway? I thought about Bob and his equipment. Wasn't he about the size of a dill pickle? I put my hands apart to demonstrate the size. "He's about, um . . ." But why should I settle for a pickle? I moved my hands farther apart. ". . . this big."

"Wow. Good for you. So you'll need the super jumbos. Now how vigorous are you in your sexual activity?"

"How vigorous?" By then, the pharmacist and I had established a nice rhythm. She would ask a simple, reasonable question, and I would respond like the village idiot. It was working out quite nicely for us.

"Yes, how vigorous. Because even though all of these condoms are adequate, some brands have a better tensile strength, which is recommended for more strenuous activity."

"Oh, of course. Tensile strength. Well, I would say that I am, er, we are very vigorous." I thought of Bob. Where would he have rated on the vigorous scale? Probably just under comatose. "Very highly vigorous."

The pharmacist and I continued in this manner through all of the pertinent issues. Color? Neutral, thank you. Flavor? A fruity assortment, please. Texture? Nubbly, but not too rough of course. Then came the final question.

"Okay, so how often?"

"How often what?"

"How often will you be using a condom?"

"Oh, well, every time."

"No, I mean how often per month or week or day. See, most people are not aware that condoms have a shelf life. We like to sell them in thirty-day supplies so they don't get stale."

"Stale, of course. Thirty-day supply? Well, then how about thirty?"

"Thirty."

"Well, maybe you should make that forty-five. I can always come back and get more if I run out, right?"

"Very good. Forty-five it is."

As I drove home, proud to have my package of forty-five jumbo-sized condoms on the car seat beside me, I thought about how long it would have taken to use up forty-five condoms while married to Bob. By my calculations, considering weekends and holidays, I figure at least seven and a half years.

Chapter 12

My next excursion was to the music store. Jessica had insisted that music was an absolute requirement for "increasing chi levels" and releasing "the Inner Feminine." I wasn't sure if I wanted all of that increasing and releasing, but I thought a little background music would be nice. Unfortunately, as Gwen had so rudely pointed out, I had absolutely no idea what kind of music I liked anymore.

I chose a huge local music store near my office. I'd never purchased anything for myself there. But every Christmas the kids would make out itemized lists of CDs they liked. And every Christmas I would come to this store and hand those unintelligible lists to some clerk or other who would find them totally intelligible. "Oh, sure, Frozen Gonads. We'll find them in the Trance/Trip Hop section." This store had seen me through many years of stocking stuffers, from *Barney's Greatest Hits* to *Wu Tang Clan*, so I figured they'd be able to help me figure out what I might enjoy in my New Chapter.

It was late morning on a Thursday, so the place, which was usually packed, was not very busy. The store was huge, with acres of CDs and tapes. I had no clue where to start, so I started by trying to find someone who might have a clue.

I walked up to the counter, where a nice-looking man about my age was dismantling the cash register. He had it all apart in little bits and looked at the mess as if his next tool of choice might be a sledgehammer.

"Excuse me. Do you work here?"

"Only when everything goes wrong." He looked up, paused, then gave me a 150-watt smile. "Sorry, this thing is making me pretty snarly. They're great when they work but when they don't . . ." His voice trailed off, and he shrugged his shoulders. "So how can I help you?"

He smiled that killer smile again. I wondered if he would be willing to join me at Mattresses Galore to bounce around a little.

"Well, I'd like to buy some music."

He looked around the huge, well-stocked store innocently. "Then I believe you've come to the right place. Artist? Title?"

I sighed. Here I was, once again, about to expose my complete ignorance. Oh, well, I was getting good at this.

"I don't know the artist or title. See, this is for me, and I haven't bought any music in more than twenty years. I mean, I've bought music but it was always for my kids or my husband, my ex-husband, but not for me. So I don't even really know what kind of music I like anymore. But I'm entering a new chapter of my life, so I'm trying to figure that out. That's why I'm here."

This was perhaps more information than a clerk in a music store needs to know. At least I had held myself back from explaining that I also didn't know my panty size nor the type of cheese I like. And besides, he seemed to be listening attentively. He had an intelligent face, a nice face (a very nice face, actually) and it was pleasant to have the undivided attention of a very nice, intelligent male face. Even if it was only because he was trying to figure out whether I was truly wacko or simply clueless.

"Oh. I see. So, then, you have no idea at all what kind of music you like?" He was having a hard time digesting this.

"No idea at all."

"But you do like music?"

"Oh, yes!"

"Opera? Jazz?"

"No idea."

"Right. Okay, then, so let's approach it this way. How old are you? I mean, if you don't mind my asking."

I didn't mind. I've never understood why people, women actually, avoid revealing their age. Maybe I'm not self-conscious about it because I'm no good at knowing other people's ages. If someone is within twenty years of me in either direction, I figure they are about my age. If they're not, they are either about my parents' age or about the kids' age. So what's a decade here or there?

"I'm forty-nine."

"Oh, good." He seemed genuinely relieved. I'd never gotten that reaction before. "See, I was afraid you were about ten years younger. At forty-nine, your musical ear was honed on Janis Joplin, The Doors, The Beatles, Jimi

Hendrix—the good stuff. If you were ten years younger, you would have been brainwashed by Captain and Tennille and KC and The Sunshine Band." He shuddered as if to ward off the Ghosts of Disco Past.

"So now what do you like to do when you play music?" I was pretty sure that "listen to it" was not the response he was seeking. I was starting to like this guy and did not want to sound like a complete idiot in front of him. So I came up with a clever rejoinder.

"Excuse me?" Not bad, huh? Polite, noncommittal, throws the ball back in his court. Made me sound like only a partial idiot

"I mean do you like to just sit back and relax or sing along or dance to it? Do you use it to meditate or go to sleep? Or are you looking for something to set a sexy, romantic mood?" At this he blushed before my blush could even get started. I really liked this guy.

"I guess I'd say all of those things. Though not all at the same time." That earned me one of his dazzling smiles again. I could stand around all day just trying to earn that smile.

"Well, let me make some suggestions then." He came around the counter and I could see that he was about five-ten, medium build with those broad shoulders that are so nice to nuzzle your head into. His hair was longish and flopped over his brow every so often. It was just beginning to turn gray.

I noticed that I was noticing this guy not just as a person, but as a *male* person. When had that started? In all the years that I was married, I can honestly say I never paid particular attention to the attractiveness (or not) of the men around me. As soon as I said "I do" a switch had turned off, the I'm-available-and-looking switch. It wasn't a conscious decision, just part of my DNA I guess. And since my divorce, it hadn't occurred to me to flip the switch back on.

But as I thought about it, unconsciously I must have been looking at men differently for the past couple of weeks. I remember checking out the UPS guy's legs and thinking that the bank teller had great hands. I realized that I could rank the rear ends of all the guys in my local supermarket (the butcher had the nicest buns by far). All of this activity around my New Chapter (flouncing around in sexy lingerie, reading racy how-to books, snuggling into my Universal Womb of throw pillows) must have flipped that switch into Dude Alert Overdrive.

In truth, Mr. Music Store was the first one to attract me. It's not that I hadn't seen men who were good-looking, probably even better-looking than he was. Maybe it was a chemistry thing (gosh, I wish I'd paid more attention to that subject in high school) or maybe my Tantric level was rising. Whatever it was, this guy with the aurora borealis smile was the first to, well, pique my interest.

I tried to act light and flirty, though I probably just came across as goofy. I was pretty rusty at this.

"So, um, what kind of music do you like?"

He laughed. Great laugh, great smile, cute buns—I'm in love! "It depends on my mood, I guess. I've got everything from Rossini to Coldplay in my collection." I smiled and nodded as if I had a clue who those people might be. I didn't.

"I'm sorry. I should have introduced myself. My name

is Tim." Tim. I had loved the name Tim for as long as I could remember. Of course, I could only remember the last seven minutes or so right then.

"I'm Angie." He shook my hand. Nice hands, better than the bank teller.

"So what kind of mood are you in these days, Angie? I mean, are you melancholy? Feeling upbeat?"

"I guess upbeat, adventuresome, in transition." And horny, I wanted to add. Angie Hawkins, where did that come from? Had I said it out loud? I was getting a little scary in my expanded horizons.

"Okay, so I've got some ideas. Bear with me. It may take me a little while to find what I'm looking for because I don't actually work here."

Oh, great. I probably interrupted a robbery, and the guy I've got the hots for has three store employees tied up in the back room. On the other hand, he was being very sweet about delaying the crime to assist me. True love learns to overlook tiny faults, like criminal activity.

"So if you don't work here . . . ?"

"Oh, I'm the owner. I mean, I don't work here on a regular basis. I only come in every once in a while because we're usually traveling so much."

Okay, he wasn't a felon, but this was much worse. He was part of a "we" who traveled together. I firmly clicked my Dude Alert switch off. I would not get involved with the half of a "we" under any circumstance. Sigh . . .

"Now here's what I'm thinking." We had entered the jazz section. "I doubt that you're trying to recapture your youth, right?" No, just my sanity. "So we're not going for the oldies. Instead, how about some jazz?" He pulled out

CDs of several artists that I'd never heard of: Diana Krall, Michael Buble, Norah Jones.

"A lot of these are classic jazz hits but by new artists. You know how our kids are gravitating toward the classics in our time (Three Dog Night, The Beatles, etc.)? Well, at our age, a lot of us are enjoying the classics of our parents' generation. These should handle the sing-along, dance-along, and romantic mood categories." His awesome smile hit me again. But this time it activated my "buy, buy, buy" chakra rather than my heart chakra.

Chapter 13

The big excursion that I most wanted to avoid could be avoided no longer. Parading around in my gorgeous new undies had revealed just how ungorgeous the body within them was. Also, some of the positions in the Kama Sutra (assuming I might one day want to try them) looked like they might require more flexibility than the ability to bend over and touch my knees. It was time to go to the gym.

How to choose a gym? I definitely didn't need the pre- and postmaternity classes from years past and I didn't think my new workout regime would require a twenty-four-hour facility. Based on my level of enthusiasm (or more accurately, level of resistance), if the gym was open fifteen minutes per day that would probably be plenty for me. I had never liked those pink and prissy strictly female gyms filled with those jiggle machines. (Honestly, if jiggling can really remove our lumps and bumps, why do all of the serious exercisers wear heavy-duty spandex, the most jiggle-free fabric since chain mail?) I didn't need a place that was upscale or trendy. I just wanted someplace close to home, with clean dressing rooms, adequate equipment, and preferably extremely dim lighting. And this time, I decided to get myself a personal trainer. I like the sound of that, don't you? Just like Suzanne Somers and Cindy Crawford and that woman with the metallic derriére.

I found a place that seemed perfect, the 29th Street Gym. Well, perfect except for the fact that it was a gym, which meant I'd have to stop procrastinating and actually start to exercise. My get acquainted appointment with Frank, my new personal trainer, was scheduled for 6:30 P.M. Too early to eat and digest dinner, too late to hold off entirely, I was forced to eat two Snickers bars on the way. (Not jumbo size Snickers, of course. I already considered myself to be in training.)

I steeled myself for what I knew I'd find: a bouncy, chirpy crowd of Oakland Raiders' cheerleaders, posing as legitimate exercisers, pedaling and pumping away on all of the equipment without even breaking a sweat, standing around showing off their perky behinds and Barbie doll waists. I'm convinced that gyms plant these women to remind you that you are seriously out of shape and therefore need to be on an exercise program, a *long-term* exercise program and that requires you to sign a *long-term* contract.

But when I walked through the doors of the 29th Street Gym, I didn't find the Oakland Raiders' cheerleaders but the Oakland Raiders themselves. The place was packed with a group of the largest, most muscle-bound men I'd ever seen in my life. This was a different species entirely. The men in this species may not be able to spell encyclopedia, but I'm sure they could tear the entire Britannica version with one swift rip.

The fashion statement for the group seemed to be the ripped T-shirt look. Not those T-shirts that Giorgio Armani shreds in his backroom. (*Ah, yes, a sassy little tear right here should add at least $75 to suggested retail.*) No, these T-shirts looked as if they simply could no longer stand the strain of those huge biceps and triceps and other miscellaneous 'ceps bulging out against them.

The muscular giant behind the counter smiled and gestured me toward him.

"Ma'am, you're letting in the cold air." I had been paralyzed at the doorway. Silly me, of course we couldn't let these delicate flowers catch the sniffles. I closed the door and moved forward.

"Um, I'm here to see Frank."

"Sure. Frank is in the back somewhere. You must be Angie Hawkins." Well, of course I was Angie Hawkins. Obviously everyone else in the place had names like Bubba, Igor, Billy Bob, or Tank. (Speaking of which, have you ever wondered how Arnold Schwarzenegger made it in his prior profession with a name like Arnold? It's a perfect name for a urologist or an actuary, but for a weight lifter/bodybuilder? Must have been rough.) "Frank's our head trainer. I'll go get him." Head trainer? Great, he'll be Goliath, the head of the Gaths, all six cubits and a span of him. I wondered if he'd be able to clear the doorway.

Frank definitely cleared the doorway and looked more like David of the Bible rather than Goliath. He was a slim, compact Asian man about thirty years old in a simple black sweat suit, as yet unripped by bulging muscles. "Hi,

Angie. Very nice to meet you. Why don't you come back to my office, and we'll talk about your goals."

Ah, my goals. My main goal at that moment was to explain to Frank that I had made some horrible mistake and needed to go sign up at one of those pink jiggle places.

"By the way, Angie, you picked an interesting night to come. Tuesdays tend to be for our really serious guys. I would imagine that you might feel pretty intimidated."

Hold it one minute, Buster! Intimidated? Me? Think you could handle two, count 'em two, childbirths? Or even one gynecological exam? How about if we stick you in a minivan full of seven-year-olds with behavior issues and see how you do? You want to talk about intimidation? Let's just have you attend the first day of the Half-Annual Sale at Nordstrom . . .

"No, Frank, not at all. I'm sure these gentlemen are very nice."

"Good. So, let's review your training goals."

Okay, so between you and me, here were my real training goals: to lose my saddlebags so I no longer looked like I was carrying oranges in my pockets. To elevate my buns so they no longer slapped against the backs of my knees when I walked. To tone underneath of my arms so they no longer flapped around in strong winds. And to be flexible enough to get into position number forty-seven of the Kama Sutra, just in case the opportunity to do so ever comes up.

Of course, I didn't have the nerve to say all those things, though I'm sure it would have given Frank a great story to tell for years to come. Instead, what I said was:

"Toning and flexibility."

"Good. Okay, any serious physical limitations?"

Not unless you count terminal cellulite in my buttocks. "No, I don't think so."

"And what type of workout routine are you on now?"

Let's see. I hoist myself out of bed in the morning and fluff the pillows. I spend at least fifteen minutes rubbing Spud and Alli's tummies . . .

"Well, Frank, because of a number of personal circumstances, I've not really been on a steady routine for some time now."

"That's okay. We'll start with the basics and build from there."

Over the next forty-five minutes, Frank got to see how very basic my basics were. And, because the 29th Street Gym is not very large, so did all of the Bubbas and Igors in attendance.

I lasted about three minutes on the stationary bike ("Frank, is there a way to make this thing go downhill?") and two minutes on the StairMaster ("Frank, could we try the elevator option next time?") For the strengthening exercises, Frank couldn't find weights that were light enough, so he ended up handing me matching rolls of toilet tissue to lift. The pièce de résistance came when Frank tried to position me on the exercise ball. I rolled completely over and under the thing in a move that none of the Three Stooges would ever be able to re-create.

I lay there on the floor and started to laugh. Then Frank started to laugh. Then all of the Bubbas and Igors in the place started to laugh. It was such a good belly laugh that I finally figured out where my abs had been hiding.

"Okay, Angie." Frank helped me up, wiping tears from his eyes. "I think we're done for this evening."

"Yep." I couldn't stop laughing. "That just might do it for me. See you Thursday?"

"Thursday it is."

At the door, I turned back to the gymful of Gaths, and shouted, "Good night, gentlemen!"

"G'night, Angie!" the bass chorus of giants responded. I'm sure my klutziness had made their evenings. Hey, maybe I'd found my mission in life: to provide comic relief to the physically fit.

Chapter 14

Lilah breezed into town during the first few weeks of my New Chapter. She and Jenna dropped by on their way to dinner to check up on me. They were a colorful pair, Lilah's pink curls rivaling Jenna's blue spikes, and they enthused over my metamorphosis.

"Geez, Mom! Look at this place! It looks great! You look good, too, like—what did you used to call it?—like a real dude magnet!"

"Angie dear, you are definitely looking less frumpy. And this place looks very inviting, almost ready for action, if you get my meaning."

"Well, Lilah, I . . ."

"But if I may offer a few suggestions? To be prepared for gentlemen callers, you'll want an empty glass placed discreetly by the bed."

"Gran, why would she have a glass by the bed?"

"Sweet Pea, a gentleman always removes his dentures before retiring for the evening."

Jenna's eyes widened. For a person who sports peacock

blue spikes, she is surprisingly easy to shock. "They take out their . . . ?"

"I also have a friend who keeps a supply of Viagra on hand for special occasions, but I've never found a diplomatic way to offer one to a gentleman when it becomes apparent that he could use a boost." Jenna blanched. "I love these pillows, Angie dear. Have you considered a mirror above the bed?"

"Gosh, Lilah, I can hardly stand to view myself in a regular mirror. I don't think . . ."

"Oh, pish-tush! There's an old proverb that says: 'If you're the only naked woman in the room, you're always gorgeous.' Just avoid the 'on top' position."

Jenna couldn't keep herself from asking, "The 'on top' position, Gran?"

"Sweet Pea, when you hit our age, you have to know these things. In the missionary position, your boobs may lie flat as pancakes. But when you're on top, your face falls forward and wrinkles up like one of those dried apple dolls. A face like that might scare a man right out of his firm resolve. And when his resolve goes limp, well . . ."

I rushed in to save Jenna from hearing Lilah's cures for limp resolve. "Lilah, I think those are excellent suggestions, and I'll definitely keep them in mind. But it's a bit premature at this point. I'm still just at the playing house stage."

"What do you mean, Mom?"

"Well, I might be set up as a dude magnet, but I'm not meeting any actual dudes."

"Well, Angie dear, you realize that new beaus aren't going to just show up at your doorstep, don't you?"

I hadn't really thought my project through beyond the preparation phase. But it would be nice if Mr. Right, fully screened for all sexually transmitted diseases and credit risks, would simply show up while I was gracefully draped amongst my mountain of pillows. Of course, he would have to call first to make sure my hair was washed and my legs were shaved.

"Dear, are you going out to meet new people?"

"Well, I've been meeting new people on my various excursions." I had told Jenna and Lilah about the shopping trips with my mentors and my other adventures (discreetly omitting the Great Condom Mission, of course).

"Mom, it doesn't sound like the guys at the gym are exactly your type, except in the Jessica Lange and King Kong sense perhaps."

"You mean Fay Wray," Lilah and I responded together.

"Who's Fay Wray?"

"From the 1930s version of *King Kong*."

"Oh." Jenna squinted at her grandmother and her mother as if to see across the great generational divide. "So, Mom, where do women your age actually go to meet men?" I could see Jenna's mind working. Does AARP sponsor geriatric raves? Are there singles' bars for the Social Security set?

"You know, Jenna, I don't really know where people go to meet people anymore."

"Angie dear, get it straight. It's where *women* go to meet *men* or vice versa. Be clear on your objective here. If you just wanted to meet new women friends, we could send you to knitting classes or menopause seminars. You are on a Man-Hunt."

I cringed at the idea of going on a Man-Hunt. When I was Jenna's age, especially when I was still in school, eligible men seemed to be wandering around everywhere. And I guess it was generally accepted that we were all in the hunt. In those days, I never had to be calculating to find men. On the other hand, maybe if I had been a little more calculating back then I would have ended up marrying a jaguar rather than Bob, the three-toed sloth.

"You know, Angie, I've met most of my recent suitors at funerals."

"Funerals, Gran?"

"Oh yes. But then I do look outstanding in black, and not all women do. Angie, how do you look in black?"

"Uh, not too bad I think, Lilah. But I don't really know that many people dying right now."

"Really? Too bad. Well, I suppose you could attend funerals of people you don't know and see how it goes. Go for the open casket ones; I've always had my best success at those."

"Maybe we need to get creative, Mom." Jenna seemed a little squeamish with the funeral idea. "I heard this morning commute radio program. If you see some guy in traffic who looks hot, you call the station on your cell phone and give them his license plate number. They announce it, and if he's listening to the same program and calls in, they connect the two of you right then."

"Sweet Pea?"

"Yes, Gran?"

"Do you seriously think your mother should go cruising for dudes in a minivan?"

"Oh. I see your point. Probably not."

"Look, I'll just check with Gwen and Jessica and Marie. They'll have some ideas." Hopefully, ideas that won't involve viewing dead people or announcing my pitiful quest for a date on the air.

That evening I e-mailed my three mentors with the critical question: *Where do old fogies like us go to meet eligible men?*

Prompt as always, their replies went something like this:

Marie: Attend community social events, interesting seminars

Gwen: Get on an Internet dating site; recruit everyone you know to set you up with blind dates

Jessica: Take up men-friendly hobbies like white-water rafting and spelunking

To properly evaluate these options, I devised a sophisticated ranking system with two categories: *Well, Maybe,* and *Not on Your Life.* After careful consideration, which lasted all of thirteen seconds, I found that most of my mentors' recommendations fell into the *Not on Your Life* category, Marie's suggestion being the only one to make it to *Well, Maybe.* I gave her a call the next day.

"So you're ready to go out and play in the real world, Angie?"

"I'd say I'm hovering halfway between dread and excitement about it, Marie. But I think it's time I tried out the New Angie in public, don't you?"

"Definitely. Let me see what's coming up." Marie works as a fund-raiser for a consortium of nonprofits in the area. Part of her job is to network by attending business events and fund-raisers of other nonprofits, so she keeps a database of all upcoming functions. She had taken me along to a few of them; some were fun, others pretty boring. But they definitely had scads of men in attendance.

"Here's one. How does this sound? There's a benefit for the Artists Guild tomorrow night, a reception and art show featuring new local talent."

That didn't sound too bad. I could stand around viewing art while exuding my newly developed magnetism and just let the eligibles come to me. Not quite as convenient as Mr. Right showing up at my doorstep, but this plan had the benefit of not having to vacuum the house in preparation.

"I wasn't planning to go because Jack and I leave for our cruise later that night. But I can show up with you, Angie, to get you launched, then leave early." That sounded okay, too. By the time Marie left, I'm sure I would be working my way through all of the Mr. Maybes surrounding me.

Chapter 15

By the next evening, the scale had definitely tipped from optimistic excitement to dread. Marie came by early to help me pick out an outfit.

"Most people will be coming straight from the office, so show me a couple of your work outfits." I pulled out my terry-cloth bathrobe and my red sweatpants with an oversized lumberjack shirt. "Angie, I think you've been working from home too much lately." She rooted through my closet and came up with a pink silk blouse, gray skirt, and jacket. I put them on, with the requisite pearl earrings and necklace.

We caravaned to the event, the nose of Marie's Land Rover an inch and a half from the back bumper of the minivan so I wouldn't fall out of formation. Perhaps she was a little suspicious of my level of enthusiasm at this point. We arrived around seven, the invitation indicating that the "fun and food" started at six-thirty. The place was jam-packed with a few starving artists and a great number of well-heeled types. These were the kind of peo-

120

ple whose original art collections were probably not hung up on their refrigerators with magnets, but tastefully lit along galleries that flanked the broad hallways of their mansions.

Marie and I window-shopped for twenty minutes or so, looking at the art (most of which was by undiscovered artists who probably should have remained that way) and men (obviously, the true purpose of our attendance). Marie nudged me whenever she saw a potential candidate. "What about him? The one with the nice silver hair? Or that guy with the sweater?"

I had been guy-gazing for the past few weeks, but not with the intention to "buy." So I didn't know exactly what I was looking for. I remembered Tim from the music store. What was it about him that I had liked? I think it was the whole package that had attracted me, not a particular look. This was going to be harder than I first thought.

Finally, Marie announced that she had to head home and pack. "I've got to talk to a few people at this thing before I go. But I'm pushing you out of the nest now, baby bird."

Ack! I wasn't ready to give up my pool floaties just yet. "Marie, maybe I should go with you . . ."

"Angie, I know this is uncomfortable, but you've got to start getting out, seeing and being seen. I want you to promise me that you'll stay for at least another hour. Promise?"

I promised the same solid kind of promise I give my dental hygienist at every checkup (*Of course I'll floss twice a day every day!*)

"Angie, think of this as practice, just practice, okay?"

When she left my side, my immediate impulse was to bolt. I am not naturally very good at these walk-around-with-your-wine-and-nibble-hors-d'oeuvres events. For one thing, I am an incorrigible wine spiller. No matter what the shape of the glass, how full or how empty, I am certain to slop it over the edges onto my clothes or, worse, onto someone else's (and I've got the dry-cleaning bills to prove it). In fact I'm sure that my preference for white wines has less to do with taste than the superior conceal-ability of white wine dribbles.

Also, I am not particularly good at striking up conver-sations with strangers. I marvel at people like Jessica who, within a three-floor elevator ride, can exchange busi-ness cards with seven new friends. "A stranger is just a friend you haven't met." Ha! A stranger is someone who doesn't know what a doofus you are until you expose it by speaking!

But Marie was right; I needed to stick it out. I'd read some tips from *The Rules* in preparation for this evening. According to the authors, the secret to success at events such as these was to flit like a butterfly, never landing in one spot for too long. *One must look happy, interested, and mysterious. Keep moving, circling the room with a wonderful carefree smile on your face.*

So I flitted and circled for about twelve minutes, my smile muscles ready to go into spasm with the effort. I passed the same candidates seven or eight times and started giving them names. There was Tall Academic, Bearded Guy, Mr. Purple Tie. My discomfort was in-creasing rather than decreasing, and my carefree smile had gotten stuck to my teeth. Surely someone would call

Security soon and have "the deranged-looking lady who keeps casing the joint" removed by force. This couldn't possibly be right. Was there a chapter in *The Rules* I missed?

I stopped in front of an odd-looking sculpture, my butterfly wings completely wilted. My brain busied itself with compelling questions. A) What would possess someone to create something so ugly, and what the heck is it supposed to be? And B) where the heck is the nearest exit so I can retreat without appearing to be the hopeless wallflower that I truly am? I couldn't see Marie but hoped she had already gone and would not catch me in my cowardly retreat.

"You come here often?" A deep male voice at my elbow startled me into spilling my wine. An experienced wine spiller, I shifted just enough so the wine missed my blouse and poured into my shoes. In true *Rules* fashion, I was ready with my clever reply.

"Huh?" I turned to find Mr. Purple Tie looking at me with a bright smile and clear blue eyes.

"I know. Dumb thing to say, isn't it? But I never know how to approach a beautiful woman at something like this. So I just say something particularly stupid in hopes she'll take pity on me and keep the conversation going."

I'm pretty sure that was my cue to speak next but I was still trying to grasp the fact that the "beautiful woman" he was approaching meant *me*.

"Oh, yes, of course. I mean, no, I don't pity you. Really, I've heard a lot worse." He laughed a gentle laugh, as if I'd said something quite charming.

"I'll bet you have. I'll bet you hear bad pickup lines all

the time." Pickup lines? Me? I was getting picked up? Wow . . .

"Here, let's go fill your glass. It's looking pretty empty." Well, of course it was, because most of what had been in my glass was by then puddled in my left shoe. Mr. Purple Tie took my elbow and steered me through the crowd to the bar in the far corner. I made slight sloshing noises as we walked.

"Would you like more of what you were having or would you prefer to try something really special?"

"Well, okay, I'll try the something special, please."

"Ah, an adventuresome woman!" He touched my hand and looked deeply into my eyes. "Whenever I have the option, I always choose something special as well."

I'm sure I felt at least four of my chakras spring wide open. As I tried to restart my breathing (in out, in, out, remember?), he turned to the bartender.

"I brought a bottle of Pinot Grigio from my home cellar. It should be waiting in the back for me."

His own wine cellar? He tipped the bartender, grabbed the opened bottle and two glasses, and gestured toward the patio.

"Shall we? I was hoping I would find someone extraordinary to share this with tonight. It's a Pinot Grigio. I hope you'll like it."

Of course I would like it! Its owner had called me both beautiful and extraordinary within the last four minutes. As a bonus, the wine was the perfect color for spilling. "So, lovely lady, what shall we drink to?"

My brain was starting to re-engage. "How about to new adventures?"

He laughed again, a very easy, pleasant laugh. "Perfect. To new adventures."

I surreptitiously studied my companion as we toasted. About five-eight, nice head of salt-and-pepper hair, very well cut suit, and expensive-looking shoes. I recognized his tie as a Hermès, only because Marie and I had hunted for one for Jack last Valentine's Day. Those ties were not cheap. My companion was obviously not one of the starving artists represented but one of their patrons.

The patio was much less crowded than the crush inside the gallery, and the evening was cool and pleasant. The Pinot Grigio was crisp and light, and my companion was much nicer to look at than the efforts of the undiscovered talent. The night had definitely taken a turn for the better.

"I'm afraid I didn't catch your name."

"I'm Angie. Angie Hawkins." I paused for him to offer his own. Nothing. "Um, and I didn't catch yours."

He laughed again. It occurred to me that he might be a little nervous also. "I'm Ben Waters. Very, very nice to meet you, Angie Hawkins." He took my hand in both of his and held it for a heartbeat. At least, I think it was a heartbeat. I wouldn't know exactly because I think mine had stopped beating right about then. My chakras were absolutely zinging and popping in all directions.

"So who are you, Angie Hawkins? Tell me about yourself. I want to know everything."

And so we talked. My brain had decided to join the party, so it was a very pleasant conversation. I talked about my kids and my work. He talked about his hobbies and his parents. I told him about my first dance recital, he told me about his first touchdown. We reminisced about the fireflies and thunderstorms of our childhoods, both of us having grown up in the Midwest. It wasn't one of those "what do you do for a living, where did you go to school" kind of conversations where you get all of the stats of a person but end up knowing very little. This conversation went all over the place. The stories we told each other revealed who we were rather than what we were.

I couldn't remember the last time I had felt this way: attractive, interesting, desirable. Ben made me feel all of those things. He was attentive and endearingly curious about me. I started feeling so relaxed with him that I hardly spilled a drop of the delightful Pinot Grigio.

Finally, Ben looked down at his watch and jumped up with a start. "Oh, no! I was supposed to check in at home hours ago. I'm really late and must run." Instantly, my awkwardness returned. "Angie, I really hate to end this." He sounded very sincere and looked a little anxious.

"Well, it has been very nice meeting you." I stood and offered my hand.

He took my hand in both of his again. Pop, pop, pop! "Angie, I know these are unusual circumstances. But you've proven yourself to be adventuresome. Would you have dinner with me next week? Maybe Wednesday evening?"

"Wednesday evening? Sure, I'd love to." *The Rules* would have said that I should have hesitated, checked my Palm Pilot, put him off for a little longer. But my newly opened chakras had taken over and were responding very enthusiastically.

"Great! Now I really do have to run. I'll call you." He

kissed me lightly on the cheek and disappeared into the gallery crowd.

I stood on the patio basking for a few minutes. I, Angie Hawkins, had just spent a delightful three-quarters of an hour with an attractive man. And I, Angie Hawkins, was going on my first date in almost thirty years!

Chapter 16

Of course, by the next morning my "I've got a date" euphoria had been replaced by a Code Blue Wardrobe Emergency. I called Jenna.

"Mom? What's wrong?" It was 6:00 A.M. and perhaps a tad too early to be calling on a Saturday morning.

"Nothing, sweetie. I've got a date."

"That's terrific, Mom, just terrific." Her enthusiasm was muffled by a yawn. "When? Tonight?"

"No, Wednesday."

"Gosh, a Wednesday night date. Well, that's, um unique. So why don't I call you when I get up, and you can tell me all about it?" This was a subtle hint that I completely ignored.

"But, Jenna, I have nothing to wear!"

A silence on the other end of the line. Every woman recognizes "I've got nothing to wear" as the universal distress signal, not to be taken lightly. I could tell Jenna was slowly pulling herself together.

"Okay, Mom. Take it easy. Where's Auntie Marie?"

"She and Jack are on a cruise until Friday."

"Gwen? Jessica?"

"Both out of town on business all week."

Jenna took a deep breath, a secure-the-lifeboats kind of breath. "So, it's just you and me?"

"Yes, sweetie." Barbara Bush and Queen Latifah.

"Okay, we can handle this. Let me throw on some clothes and wash my face. Put on some coffee, Mom, and stay calm. The cavalry is coming."

The cavalry showed up looking naturally lovely in a faded lavender sweat suit, white tank top, and tennies. She gave me a kiss on the cheek and grabbed a cup of coffee.

"Okay, Mom, I've been thinking this through on the way over. You and I don't typically gravitate toward the same types of clothes, do we?" This was understatement in the extreme.

"No, sweetie. I know we don't."

"But a sense of real style supersedes any particular trend or fashion preference, doesn't it?"

"Uh, I guess so."

"And I have always had a great sense of style, haven't I?"

"Well, yes, that certainly is true." Even as a toddler, she seemed to have an extraordinary sense of style, her little Huggies drooping below her color-coordinated playsuit. She stopped letting me dress her as soon as she could stand long enough to pull something out of her drawers.

"So, Mom, all I have to do to get the right outfit for you is to think of this as a hunt for a period costume. Something stylish, but not of this era, right?"

"Ah, so you'll just think of me as a relic of a bygone period? Kind of like Scarlett O'Hara? Wilma Flintstone?"

"Exactly!" She was so sincere and enthusiastic that I couldn't take offense. Besides, Jenna was my only hope.

"So, Mom, we'll start by defining this date." She pulled out a pad and pen. "When is he picking you up?"

"I don't know."

"Okay, then where are you going?"

"Out to dinner."

"Where?"

"I don't know."

"Well, what kind of place?"

"I don't know."

"Mom, you've got to work with me here. Think. Based on your knowledge of the man . . . what's his name?"

"Ben."

"Good name. Ben. Based on your knowledge of Ben, what kind of place do you think he might choose?"

I thought about Ben's well-cut suit, expensive-looking shoes, Hermès tie, and the Pinot Grigio from his very own wine cellar.

"A nice place. Probably a very nice place with good food and expensive wines."

"All right! Now we're getting somewhere! So it needs to be a nice outfit that can be dressed up or casualed down at the last minute, good for either early-evening or late-night dining." Jenna jotted it all down, and I began to relax in the presence of her calm competence. I wondered if she had this same soothing effect on her bovine patients.

"Next, how much do you like this guy?"

"Um, I don't really know."

"But you do like him, right? You're not just going out

with him as a sympathy date, hoping you'll never have to see him again?"

"Good grief, no!"

"Good, because that would be a different outfit entirely."

"There's an outfit specifically for getting rid of a guy?"

"Of course, Mom. It looks just like most of the clothes in your closet." I must have looked crushed because Jenna laughed and put her arm around me. "I'm just kidding, Mom! For goodness sakes, lighten up! It's just a date."

I pointed out to Jenna that the last real date I'd been on had been nearly a decade before she was born. That seemed to put it into perspective for her.

"Wow. Then I guess you're entitled to be a little uptight. Let's just focus on having you look good for that night. It always helps me through the first date with someone. So here's the key question: What's the message you're trying to put across? The sound bite, what your clothes should say to your date?"

"Message? Sound bite?"

"Mom, clothes are just packaging. What's inside is the product, *you*, who you *really* are. But clothes are used to get some message about the you inside across to the consumer, in this case Ben."

Jenna had taken a semester of marketing in college and did very well as I recall. I began to feel like a box of macaroni.

"You mean like 'microwaveable'?"

"Or how about 'Contents may be partially frozen'?"

After considering messages like "Keep right side up" and "Available to a good home," we decided that "Cook over slow flame for best results" would be the outfit's slogan.

"So, Mom, shall we see what's in your closet that might work?"

We looked at each other, one of those mother-to-daughter moments of truth. "Jenna, there is absolutely nothing in my closet that would work." She nodded solemnly. "I've got work clothes and clean the house clothes. I've got go to the gym and the grocery store clothes. I've still got clothes that are good for going to soccer games and PTA meetings, even though I haven't needed those for a while. But I don't have anything, anything at all to wear on any kind of a date, not even a date to go bowling! My clothes are all tucked in, tidy, tailored, and boring!"

"Mom, you're right." Couldn't she have paused a second longer before agreeing with me? "But then again, the life you've led has been pretty tucked in, tidy, tailored, and boring up to this point, hasn't it? The good news is that you raised two absolutely brilliant and adorable children during that dismal phase of your life." She grinned broadly. "And now one of your brilliant, adorable children is here to help get you all dressed up and ready for your exciting new chapter! Just like playing Barbie dolls!"

The phone rang, and Jenna leaped for it. "Oooo, maybe it's him, Ben!"

"Jenna, don't you dare."

"Hello? Well, yes, she's here but I don't know if I should let you talk to her."

"Jenna!"

"Relax, Mom, it's Tyler. Tyler, guess what? Mom's got a real date! And she wants me to help her find a supersexy outfit . . ."

"Jenna!"

"No, I haven't met him. No, I don't know. Here talk to her yourself." She handed me the phone. "Watch out, Mom. He's going into that superprotective male mode."

"Tyler? How are you, honey?" In the midst of my pre-date wardrobe panic, I'd completely forgotten our traditional Saturday morning call.

"So, Mom, what's this about a date? How come I haven't heard about this guy before? Have you known him for very long? What's his name? How old is he? Where does he live? What does he do for a living?" Tyler's voice had a little too much intensity in it for mere curiosity. I could imagine him filing an FBI report on Ben.

I answered his questions as well as I could, glossing over the fact that actually I knew few facts about Ben and had only known him for a total of forty-five minutes.

"So, honey, when are you coming home?"

"Well, we submit the article a week from Monday and I'm sure we'll be working down to the wire. I'll pack up the apartment on Tuesday and fly in Wednesday. My interview with Judge Bennett is scheduled for Friday, which is Halloween. Do you think I should wear my Ghostbusters costume?" I smiled. I had made Tyler a Ghostbusters costume for Halloween the year he was six. For the next three years, he refused to wear anything but that costume, believing that it was the source of his incredibly good candy hauls. So we lowered the pant legs and lengthened the sleeves until they could be lowered and lengthened no more. He swore that the quality of candy was never as good after that.

"Shall Jenna and I find you an appropriate interview outfit to wear while we're out today?"

He laughed, a very tired I've-been-working-much-too-hard-lately kind of laugh.

"I'll take a pass, Mom. Have fun and don't let Jenna talk you into any tattoos or anything. I love you, Mom."

"I love you, too, Tyler."

Chapter 17

Jenna and I had not shopped for clothes together since she was fourteen. At that time we determined that it would be easier on her nerves and my blood pressure if we confined my role to supplying the credit card at the end of a shopping excursion. Our shopping styles were as different as our taste in clothes. Jenna was focused, swift, decisive. She did most of her culling outside of the dressing room, inspecting each item with a critical eye. In fact, so few items actually passed her inspection that she never had much to try on. But for the most part, she ended up buying things she tried on. I, on the other hand, tended to wander around, picking clothes off of this rack and that, filling every hook, doorknob, and bench in a dressing room with all the clothes I wanted to try on. And I usually ended up buying none of it.

Due to the urgency of this particular shopping trip, Jenna took the lead and marched us into Nordstrom. For the first twenty minutes, I went from rack to rack, pulling out clothes for Jenna's reaction. "No, not your color." "No, too cutesy." "No, bad shape for you." She finally got tired of explaining, and just said, "No." I decided to give my biceps a rest and just follow her around.

Jenna was like a cunning huntress, moving slowly and systematically through the jungle of racks, her eyes taking in every detail as she moved. Every so often she pounced on some garment and pulled it out for closer scrutiny. She scrunched the fabric in her hand, turned the item this way and that to catch it in different lights. She held it up in front of me squinting her eyes, then flipped it around to see how it moved. Only one in twenty passed all her tests. After an hour and a half, we entered the dressing room with just three outfits for consideration.

I stripped, and Jenna commented approvingly on my upgraded new lingerie. "Very 'ooh la la,' Mom. So, try on the blue first."

She handed me a royal blue jumpsuit. It had three-quarter sleeves, a deep V-neck with collar, a wide belt and slim pant legs. Its fabric had a slight sheen to it, and it was stunning.

"Beautiful, Mom! The color overpowers you a little bit, but that's just because your makeup is so blah. Try moving around in it."

I walked, quite elegantly I thought, around the dressing room. "No, Mom, really move." She made me sit, squat, do a little can-can.

"Jenna, I doubt I'll need to be quite so athletic on this date."

"Oh, I know. But you want to feel free, like you could do whatever you want, be spontaneous. You don't want clothes that confine you."

"Well, I feel like I could do anything in this! It's wonderful!"

"Good. So now try the cream."

The cream was an above-the-knee sweater dress of soft angora. The dress itself was a turtleneck, slim and sleeveless, and it had a matching long-sleeved duster. If you ignored the fact that I hadn't shaved my legs in a month or two, it looked gorgeous on me.

"Awesome! Looks elegant yet huggable. How does it feel?"

"Delicious!" I did my can-can and squat routine. I felt almost giddy with how good I looked in not one, but two different outfits!

"Okay, Mom. Now the brown."

Jenna's last find was a chocolate brown ankle-length dress in a slinky knit fabric. It had a sweeping boat neck, long sleeves, and a side slit that came up to midthigh. The dress clung to my body in ways I've never allowed a dress to cling before.

"Wow!" Jenna grinned in the mirror behind me. "Kid, you got potential!"

"Oh, Jenna, these all look wonderful! I've never found one outfit that looks this good, much less three! How will I ever decide which one to buy?"

"Mom, let me ask you something. Do you think that Wednesday night will be the very last date you ever have in your entire life?"

"Good grief! I should hope not!"

"Then I say, better to be prepared." She grinned again. "Get all three."

Jenna and I proceeded to find scarves, belts, shoes, and

jewelry to ensure that all three outfits could be dressed up or down. We exited the store, arms loaded with packages. I hope our lucky salesclerk worked on commission; if so, after our little shopping trip she could certainly put all of her children through college.

Chapter 18

As we approached Jenna's car in the lot, she turned as if inspired. "Mom! Have your ever considered doing something about your hair?'

"Like what?"

"Well, like color or something."

I looked up at Jenna's peacock blue spikes. "Sweetie, I just don't think I'm ready to go there."

"Oh, I don't mean like my kind of color, though you might look nice in a lime green. I was thinking more like highlights or something."

"Gregory thinks I should just stay natural." Gregory had been cutting my hair for fifteen years. And for fifteen years, it had looked pretty much the same. Mousy brown, straight chin-length bob with bangs.

"Mom, Gregory is not only lazy but totally without imagination!" Déjà vu. Jenna had made this very same statement when, at age ten, she had refused to ever let him cut her hair again. "He's a barber!" The ultimate insult.

"Well, I guess it wouldn't hurt to look into it."

"Mom, why don't we just drop by and see the guy who does my hair and see what he says?"

"Well, I don't know, sweetie . . ."

"Come on, Mom. Isn't this your new chapter of life?"

"Well, okay, but won't we need an appointment?"

"No, Grok likes me very much. He'll fit us in."

Grok? I was going to get hair advice from a person named Grok? As Jenna called Grok's number from her cell phone, I got a clear image of Ben, opening my door on Tuesday night and seeing me in my luscious new cream sweater dress—with a rainbow-colored Mohawk.

"Great! Grok rescheduled another appointment so he can fit us in." Oh, yippee skippee! What would a Grok look like? Tattoos, metal-studded dog collar? Would he use shears or maybe just his razor-sharp switchblade that had seen more violent action.

The reality, fortunately, did not come close to my imaginings. Jenna led me through the doors of a shiny, trendy, upscale salon that was bustling on this Saturday afternoon. Grok turned out to be Garrauch, a chic Frenchman with silver temples and an equally silver tongue.

"Ah, my Jen-jen, *ma petite jeune fille!*" He kissed her hand smoothly, which she accepted as an everyday occurrence. "Why did you not tell me you had such a lovely *maman?*" As he reached for my hand, I scrunched my fingers inward, hoping he wouldn't notice the sorry state of my nails. The resulting fist nearly bopped him in the nose. "Please. Let us talk." With a graceful gesture, he led us to his station in the back of the salon.

Garrauch's station was larger than the rest and very well appointed, probably denoting his place in the hairstylists' hierarchy. He sat me in his chair, turned me toward the mirror, and ran his fingers through my hair. "Ach, ach." I was pretty sure from his doleful expression that "ach" was not a good sign. He turned to Jenna standing nearby. "Such a naturally lovely woman. But her hair! It is dead, *n'est-ce pas*? How very, very sad!"

The two of them talked over me in hushed tones, and I felt like a comatose patient on a gurney in the emergency room.

"Doctor, is there any hope for the patient?"

"Well, nurse, I don't think so. Maybe we should just pull the plug."

"No, no!" the patient screams silently. "I'm alive in here."

Jenna looked anxious. "But, you can do something for her, can't you, Garrauch? She has a very important date on Wednesday."

He sighed as only Frenchmen are taught to do. I think Prometheus, who had it pretty rough, invented that sigh. But the French inherited it somehow and have kept it to themselves ever since.

"Perhaps." Another sigh. "But"—he spun me around and, nose to nose, looked piercingly into my eyes—"you must trust me implicitly, madam. No questions, no fear."

"Oh, okay." Could I ask for general anesthesia? A blindfold? He offered a glass of wine instead, which I gratefully accepted.

I can't exactly describe what happened over the next two and a half hours. Garrauch and Jenna conferred about my course of treatment in whispers. Then I heard a lot of snipping noises, though I didn't see much hair falling off. Garrauch plunked a holey shower cap on my head and poked around with crochet needles, tinfoil, and white gooey foam. After that was done, he rolled my hair in a hodgepodge pattern of pink rollers, squirted some odd-smelling lotion on them, and put me under the dryer to cook.

Jenna headed out to get us sandwiches while I sat under the dryer and a pretty young woman named Celeste approached with her mobile manicure station. "Jenna sent me over to do your nails, Mrs. Hawkins."

Uh-oh, my nails. I had worn nail polish only once in my life, for my cousin's wedding. My nails had been painted a bright salmon color to match the bridesmaids' outfits, and I had felt silly, like a little girl with a Tinker Bell cosmetic kit. My fingers are small and stubby, my nails kept short through conscientious nibbling. I just didn't think I was the fancy polish type.

"Shall we try for the natural look? Maybe a subtle French nail?" Bless you, Celeste! She smoothed on base coat, ridge filler coat, pink sheen coat, tiny moon slivers of white, then finally a top coat. "This should last until the big date on Wednesday but I'll send you home with the supplies just in case." That was very sweet of her, but there was absolutely no chance that I'd remember which coat to paint where, and those tiny white slivers were completely beyond my paint-by-numbers talent.

Finally, the arduous treatment to resuscitate my dead locks was coming to a close. An exhausted-looking Garrauch asked me to close my eyes while he completed the blow-drying.

"And, now, madam, *voilà*!" He spun me toward the mirror with a flourish. Garrauch, Jenna and I stared at my reflection in the mirror. My hair was . . . spectacular! It looked quite easy and natural, with soft highlights, a slight wave, and a bounciness that I had never seen before. Tears welled up in all three sets of eyes.

"Garrauch! How can I ever thank you?!"

"Ah, madam." He wiped his eyes soulfully. "Your radiance is my reward. I will cherish the memory."

Along with the cherished memory of my radiance, I left Garrauch a very large tip.

By the time Jenna and I reached home, it was nearly dusk. We were both exhausted from our strenuous efforts to turn me from Aging Soccer Mom into Bodacious Babe. Spud and Alli gave us a rousing welcome of beagle bays as we carried in the packages. Jenna arranged my new outfits in the closet while I fed my obviously starved (and more obviously spoiled) pups.

"I'm wiped out, Mom. So I'll head home. I was thinking about Wednesday though. I'm supposed to assist with the artificial insemination of a large herd most of next week, and I'm not sure I'll be done in time to help you get dressed. But if you need me . . ."

"Don't worry, sweetie. I think I can dress myself. And I'd hate for you to miss the insemination of the herd. I'm sure it will be a life-changing event for you." (It certainly would be for me.)

"I love you, Mom." She hugged me with one of those great hugs that makes all the stretch marks and labor pains she gave me worthwhile.

"I love you, too, Jenna. And thank you. You're a real friend."

Chapter 19

That next morning I was puttering around when I got a call from Gwen, who was in New York for a deposition.

"Angie? Can you hear me?" She was on a cell phone, and the connection was not great.

"Yes. I can hear you. Gwen, I've got a date!"

"A what? What have you got?"

"A date! I've got a date with a man I met!"

"Oh, a date! Good for you! What's his name?"

"Ben. Ben Waters."

"Walter? That's great! What are you going to wear?"

Screaming, as if that would solve our static problem, I explained that Jenna had handled the fashion aspect.

"And what about makeup? Did she help you with that? Angie, you need to do something about your makeup. It's abysmal! Look this connection is really bad. Just fix your makeup, okay?" Click.

Argh! Now what? There's a perfectly good reason why my makeup is abysmal. I don't know how to apply it, and

I have a phobia about cosmetic consultants. The last time I had a makeover was sometime during the Carter administration. The woman who did it insisted that my eyebrows had been plucked beyond redemption and that my pores were the size of moon craters. But she worked hard to make me look good, disguising my many flaws as she enumerated them. By the time she was done with me, I looked great. But I knew I would never be able to re-create what she had done and slinked out of the store with my self-esteem banished to Siberia.

I'm sure that the mission statement of the International Cosmetic Counter Ladies Union is to ensure that every woman in America has at least one cupboard overflowing with tiny little tubes of cosmetics that cost a fortune and require a Ph.D. in makeupology to apply. Every once in a while, I'll brave going to my local department store cosmetic department to get the free gift offered. Over the years, I'd estimate that each "free" tube of lipstick has cost me an average of $437.00.

Another thing about cosmetic counter ladies (did I mention I have a phobia?) is that they themselves are perfect-looking. Not a hair out of place, no leaking lipstick lines, no dog hairs on their crisp, colorful smocks. They're able to look good even under fluorescent lights. There's something abnormal about that, like the Stepford wives. How can you trust such a person?

I remembered that Gwen had included *Makeup for Dummies* on her list, so I hunted and found it in the stack. How hard could this be? Gorgeous models with the IQs of celery sticks can apply makeup. So, why not me?

I flipped through the first pages and realized that another shopping trip was in order. Brushes, foundation, powders, lip liners—the list of tools and paints was a long one. But if I was serious about come-hither eyes and kiss-me-quick lips, clearly I needed to be properly equipped.

Okay, I could do this. Armed with the list of tools from the *Dummies* book and my sternest don't-you-dare-try-to-sell-me-anything look, I headed to Macy's. The perfect-looking woman behind the cosmetic counter was very attentive as I read her my list.

"*Makeup for Dummies*, right?"

"Uh, as a matter of fact, yes. How did you know?"

"Because my eleven-year-old daughter just got that book and asked for the same items." She looked at me, arching one perfectly plucked eyebrow, her flawlessly outlined lips pursed in concentration. "Let's be perfectly honest with each other, shall we?"

I'm pretty sure that I've never been *perfectly* honest with anyone, operating under the theory that perfect honesty can be dangerous. Perfect honesty can get you kicked out of school ("So, Angela, what do you think of Keats's 'Ode on a Grecian Urn'?"), fired ("Angie, don't you think my nephew will make a great addition to the team?"), and possibly ruin your marriage ("Angie, do you think I look okay in these bicycle shorts?" Okay, so in retrospect, I could have been perfectly honest on that one: "No! You look like 265 pounds of sausage about to be squeezed out of its casing!").

So my reply to the perfect-looking cosmetic counter lady was with less-than-perfect honesty. "Sure, we can be perfectly honest."

"Well, then let's just admit that you are afraid of me and intimidated by the whole arena of cosmetics."

"I am?"

"Yes. You're certain that if I give you a makeup session, I will not only try to sell you everything in the store but that by tomorrow, you won't remember how to apply it, right?"

"Well, no, not exactly."

"Uh-huh. Not exactly what?"

"The tomorrow part. I won't be able to remember by the time I hit the parking lot."

"I see. My name is Doris, Ms . . . what is your name?"

"Hawkins. Angie Hawkins."

"Ms. Hawkins, you appear to be a woman of at least average intelligence, are you not?"

"Well, yes, I . . ."

"You are able to dress yourself? Balance your checkbook? Drive a car?"

"To a certain extent, yes, but . . ."

"Ms. Hawkins. I am a professional. I could merely sell you those items on your list and be done with it. But when I see a face like yours, which has so much potential . . ."

"It does?"

"Oh, yes! Good bone structure, relatively unscathed by time, even proportions. There is no reason why your makeup should detract from your features as it does. As a professional, the solutions to your makeup problems are so obvious to me. I am dying to take just fifteen minutes and give you the look you deserve."

"Doris, can't I just buy my brushes and go?"

She sighed a huge *Why me, Lord?* sigh. "Very well. As you wish." She sighed again poignantly. Wasn't there some children's story about a monster, a very nice mon-

147

ster, who was terribly sad because all of the children were afraid of him? I can't remember how it ended. Perhaps I was being unfair.

"Well, okay, Doris, maybe we could . . ."

"Great! I know just how we should get started! Let's first try this cleanser . . ."

So forty-five (*not* just fifteen) minutes later, I left the store with absolutely every cosmetic, antiwrinkle cream, and cleanser Doris could have possibly sold me. Having, of course, absolutely no idea how to reapply any of it.

Chapter 20

The next few days were agonizingly slow. I tried to concentrate on work but found myself drifting off into fantasies of what-if. What if Ben turns out to be Mr. Right? What if we fall madly in love Wednesday and decide to get married? What if we are so eager to be together that we decide to marry next week? How about Halloween? We could have little pumpkins lining the aisle and . . .

"You want to do the asphalt job on Halloween, Angie?"

"What?" I was on a conference call discussing the parking lot at one of Phil's retail centers. Curb cuts, Petromat, slurry seal—really fascinating issues.

"I asked when you wanted to repave the lot, and you said Halloween."

"The lot. Right. No. let's wait until spring." A spring wedding with daffodils and . . .

Good grief, what was I thinking? After talking to this man for less than an hour, I was ready to order our monogrammed towels. Mrs. Ben Waters. Angie Waters. Has a nice ring to it, doesn't it? Good grief! He's an attractive man, but I was thinking like a thirteen-year-old with a bad, bad crush. Prince Charming dreams are as hard to kill as crabgrass. No matter how many husbands betray us, no matter how many boyfriends take advantage of us, no matter how many frogs still remain frogs after we kiss them, we still want to believe that maybe, just maybe, that next one is The One. And who knows? Maybe Ben would turn out to be The One, but I was certainly getting ahead of myself.

All of my best friends were out of town, and Jenna was knee deep in artificial inseminations (if that's the part of the anatomy that gets deep in those situations). So I had no one to talk me down from this nervous high anticipating my date with Ben. Instead, I heard from all of the men in my life. Don't get me wrong, I appreciate the men in my life. But, honestly, who would you rather have in the delivery room with you? Your husband, the guy in the corner who has turned green and mumbles a pathetic "How you doin', hon?" every ten minutes or so? Or your mom or your sister or your best friend, who sits right on the bed and grabs your hand, breathing and screaming with you through it all? Yeah, me, too. But this time, by default, I heard from my guys.

Marvin: "So, Angie, how is our little spending plan working out? Have you been able to put a little into savings this month?"

"Well, not really, Marvin. I've had some expenses come up. Some things that you could call 'basic equipment' for this new life I'm living."

"Oh, like some home exercise equipment? An alarm

system for your apartment? A new computer? That kind of thing?"

"Uh, yes, that kind of thing." And lacy thongs and condoms and sexual how-to books . . .

"Great, Angie! I'm glad you're spending a little to take care of yourself. But please check in with me every once in a while. I get worried when I don't hear from you."

Phil: "So, Angie, have you figured out what inspires you? What opportunity you want to seize at this moment?"

"Um, I think so, Phil. I'm trying to make some new connections."

"Very good. Networking can always bring in new ideas, new ventures, new projects."

"Yes, well, these connections are of a more personal nature."

"Oh. As in a male personal nature?"

"Actually, yes. I'm going on a date."

"I see." Phil paused, obviously choosing his next words carefully. "I only wish that Susan and I could be there to meet this young man, this suitor of yours. Angie, you are a lovely young woman and deserve someone who will treat you as the precious person you are."

"Why, thank you, Phil! That's very sweet."

"It's just that I hope your taste in men has improved with time. I'm sorry to say that I never did care at all for Bob." Well, Phil, join the club.

"Don't worry, Phil. I'm just going on a first date. But if I hear wedding bells chiming, I promise you'll have every opportunity to screen my young man first."

"I would be honored."

*   *   *

Tyler: "Mom, I was thinking maybe we should go over a few things before your date."

"What kinds of things, honey?"

"Well, you haven't been out there in a long time, and we need to talk about your safety and precautions you should take." Uh-oh. I don't think I'm hip enough to handle a safe sex lecture from my son.

"My safety?"

"Yes. For instance, are you meeting in a well-lit public place? Are you driving your own car in case you feel uncomfortable and want to leave? Have you left his name and driver's license number with a friend? Told someone where you are going and when to expect you back?"

It all came back to me, the worry of having my kids out at night. The urge to stuff them back in my womb so they would be safe from the world. And when they showed up fifteen minutes late, the simultaneous impulse to strangle and hug them.

"Tyler, you sound kind of worried about this. Are you uncomfortable with me dating?"

"Oh, not at all, Mom. It's not that. It's just that you can be a little naïve about some things, know what I mean?" If Tyler had seen my new library, he might have reconsidered that statement.

"Tyler, don't worry. I've been doing my homework. I've already checked this guy out and verified that he's not a serial killer."

"You did? Good."

"Tyler, that was a joke."

"Oh." He sounded disappointed.

"Honey, I promise to be careful, okay? Don't worry about me."

"Okay. I love you, Mom."

"I love you, too, Tyler."

Jack: "Angie, can you hear me? I don't know how to work this ship-to-shore contraption. How are you?"

"I'm fine, Jack. Is everything okay?"

"Oh, yes. But I forgot to tell you that I've got a special delivery coming Wednesday or Thursday. Would you mind watching out for it?"

"Of course not, happy to do it. How's the cruise?"

"Oh, just fine. I've already sunburned my old bald pate, and I'm on my second motion sickness patch. But Marie is having a wonderful time, so it's worth it. She's having a massage right now and said to give you her love."

"Well, tell her I've got a date this week."

"Ah-ha! Now that is news! So you're jumping in with both feet, huh? Good for you! Angie, I hope you have a truly wonderful time. Tell whoever he is that he's a lucky man."

"Thanks, Jack." Jack seemed to be the only one of "my men" who didn't think that, left on my own, I would make a total mess of my life. But then again, Jack hadn't known me as long as the others had.

Bob: *Bob!* Bob and I had hardly seen each other since the divorce had become official, and we rarely talked on the phone. In those first months, one of our infrequent inter- actions could shake me up for days, upsetting whatever postdivorce composure I had gained. But eighteen months later, I had evolved to finding Bob simply annoying.

153

"So, Angie, Jenna tells me that you are seeing someone."

Dear Jenna! She loves her dad but is still irked at him for all that had happened. She uses every opportunity to tweak him when she can. "Seeing someone" was definitely an exaggeration, but I could play the game.

"Yes, I am. And your point is . . . ?"

"Well, I just want you to know, Angie, that it's okay with me."

And they say women are unfathomable? Help me out here. This was the man who left me and our twenty-six years of marriage for Double Chocolate Cream Cheese Brownies and a monthly stipend, whose marriage vow had apparently been "until debts do us part." And he's now calling to tell me that he doesn't mind if I date someone else? Well, a) I don't give a fig for what he thinks and b) it's none of his business what I do and c) . . .

"Angie, I just want you to know that I've done a lot of soul-searching over the past many months and, as far as I'm concerned, all is forgiven."

"And what exactly is forgiven, Bob?" The fact that you hit the high life with your new girlfriend while I struggled to stay afloat? The fact that you left it to me to tell our children and all of our friends and family about the divorce? The fact that you couldn't even show up to sign the final papers because you were in Cancún and couldn't disrupt your itinerary? Is that what you're forgiving?

"You know, everything. I'm ready to put the past behind us. And it sounds as if you are finally willing to make some changes and move on with your life. So I'm happy for you."

"Bob, let me be perfectly honest . . ."

"Ooops! Other line. That must be Clarisse calling to pick her up from the spa. Gotta run!" Click.

"Let me be perfectly honest, Bob, you twit, you moron, you snorer! My underwear may have been a little boring, but yours was disgusting! And you wouldn't know a Pinot Grigio from a Budweiser, you troglodyte! The beagles never liked you, and neither did anyone else! You were lucky to have me, you nitwit, and you blew it! And now my chakras are opening and my Tantric juices are flowing, so just you watch out!"

The dial tone was beginning to interfere with my harangue, so I replaced the receiver. I used my anger to do an intense set of stomach crunchies. When I was on crunchie #103, Ben called.

"Angie, it's Ben. You sound a little breathless."

"Just doing my workout." I tried to get my breath under control, but the sound of his voice had more of a breathless effect on my breathing than the crunchies had.

"It's so good to hear your voice. I've been thinking about you."

"You have?" I wondered if Ben had run out desperately shopping for a new tie, trimmed his hair, and considered a face-lift in preparation for Wednesday night. Do men do those things? I'm sure I could look it up in one of Gwen's books.

"Of course! I'm really looking forward to Wednesday night." Me too. So much so that I can barely function as an adult human being. "I was thinking I could pick you up around seven. Would that be okay?"

We talked a little longer, and I kept it light (per coaching from *The Rules*). I would have plenty of time later to grill him on the statistical information I was missing. I didn't want to sound too "interested." But I did pick up a few clues from our conversation. He had been "in court" all day, which meant he was an attorney or a judge or a traffic violator. He quoted from an old Bob Dylan song about being older then but much younger now, so I figured he was either my age or a fan of the oldies station. And the fact that we could dine at seven on a school night probably meant that he was not single-parenting any little ones at home. Tyler would have been proud of my investigative abilities.

Chapter 21

Wednesday, the Big Day, finally arrived. (Where on earth have you been? I've been waiting for you!) After a brief, very unproductive day at the office, I took myself off early and headed home. Was two-thirty too early to start dressing for a seven o'clock date?

I showered and shaved my legs, nicking myself only three times. I shampooed, conditioned, and blew my hair dry. It wasn't quite as magnificent as when Garrauch styled it, but it was pretty darn good.

My French nails had one microscopic chip in them. I couldn't get Celeste's bottle of nail polish open (are there strength requirements for manicurists?) so I opted for the bottle of Wite-Out on my desk. It took me seven minutes to steady my hand enough to get the tiny dot of white in just the right place. Then I spent the next seven minutes flapping my arms to make sure it was dry. Uh-oh. Should I reshower?

Next I tackled makeup. I laid out the thirty-seven inexplicable cosmetic products Doris had sold me and opened my *Makeup for Dummies* book to "evening looks." I foundationed and powdered my splotchy face until it was a "clean canvas." Then, with slightly darker shades, created bone structure where there was none. Is Iman really that beautiful or just a really good artist?

The tough stuff was next. I had a little trouble getting the eyebrow arch in the right place. My first attempt made me looked enraged, the second rendition came out as "astonished." I ended up settling for "mildly quizzical."

However, I am proud to say that I figured out how to create clean lines with eyeliner and lip liner. If you grip one shaking hand tightly with the other shaking hand, the opposition of their shakes results in a firm steadiness. The authors really should add that as a tip in the *Dummies* book. I crimped my lashes with the eyelash curler per instructions and applied three full coats of mascara. (Okay, so haven't you always wondered who ever thought of curling eyelashes in the first place? My theory is that many accepted beauty procedures, including plucking eyebrows, exfoliating, and waxing off lip hair, originated during that very innovative era, the Spanish Inquisition. When an idea for a new torture was rejected as not manly enough, the Spanish Inquisitors didn't want to lose their R&D investment in it. Therefore, they created Revlon as a secondary profit center.)

Earlier in the week, with great deliberation, I had chosen a "special occasion" lingerie set to wear for this evening rather than my "moment of truth" option. I was going on a date, for gosh sakes! Not preparing to leap into bed with a guy I'd only known for forty-five minutes! But just in case, where were those condoms? I found them. Now where do you put them? Leave one under the pillow like the tooth fairy? No, too premeditated. How about in the drawer by the bed? Okay, that's good. NOT that I intended on having the occasion to use them tonight. For gosh sakes, I was just going out on a date!

I decided to wear the cream sweater dress—no, no, the blue jumpsuit—no, no, the brown dress—no, no, the blue . . . After thirty-three changes, I settled for the brown ensemble because it had survived my indecisiveness with the fewest wrinkles. I put on the "dress it up" jewelry and belt Jenna and I had chosen and the "kicky little sandals." I was all ready and I looked pretty gosh darn good, if I do say so myself. It was four-forty-five.

Okay, so obviously I was out of practice and had not timed this very well. I took off the dress and hung it up carefully, put on my bathrobe, and replaced my kicky sandals with slippers. Then I did what I always do when I happen to have a little extra time. I ironed.

Ironing is a boring, soothing, mindless task. I don't like it per se, but in times when I need something to do, something that requires limited mental involvement, something to calm my nerves, ironing is perfect. And ironing is so reliable, always waiting around to be done, eager but not pushy. If they ever perfect wrinkle-free clothes, I'll have to resort to Quaaludes.

So I ironed the shirts I would be wearing for the next six or seven weeks and several pairs of cotton slacks. I ironed the shorts and sleeveless shirts that were ready to be boxed up and put into storage for winter. I ironed all of the items destined for the Salvation Army. I ironed a set of sheets and pillowcases and changed the bed—not that anyone but me would see those sheets that night. It's just a nice thing to do sometimes.

At about six-thirty, the phone rang startling me out of my ironing stupor.

"Angie! It's Ben. I'm glad you're home already. Something has come up." Oh no! Was he calling to cancel? After all of the showering and shaving and primping and ironing and . . .

"I'm in court and running a little late. So I'm having a car sent for you, okay? It'll pick you up at seven as planned and take you to the restaurant. Is this okay? I'm so sorry about this."

He's sending a car? I felt like Christina Onassis.

"Of course, I don't mind. Could you have the driver call just before he arrives to be sure I am ready?" Ha! Can you believe I said that? I was becoming very suave.

Now that I had stalled so long, engrossed in my ironing, I needed to seriously hustle and get dressed. Of course this time, I ripped my way through three brand-new pairs of stockings. I caught the zipper of my dress right at that place on your back you can only reach if you've been bred as a contortionist. I rescued myself by shinnying the dress around until the back was under my armpit. Then of course pinched my skin in the zipper as I got it released from the fabric. Only minor bleeding. I couldn't figure out why the kicky sandals felt so uncomfortable until I realized I had put them on the wrong feet. I spritzed some perfume in my left eye, causing said eye to tear up and, of course, ruin my carefully applied mascara. Ah, yes, I was becoming very suave.

I repaired all of the damage I had done to myself and, by the time the driver called to say he was out front, I looked pretty gosh darn good again—and as if I had just run a forty-yard dash.

Chapter 22

The driver was wearing a cap—a chauffeur's cap!—and standing with the back door open for me. The car was not a limo (how clichéd that would have been!) but a big black Mercedes.

"How are you this evening, miss? I'm James, and I'll be taking you to meet Mr. Waters."

"Thank you, James." James? As in "Home, James?" I tried not to giggle. But I was very, very nervous. And when I'm very, very nervous I either pee in my pants or giggle. I decided that a giggle or two would be the better choice.

"Did you say something, miss?"

"No, I was just thinking of a joke a friend told me this afternoon." My giggle was moving to guffaw level.

"And what joke would that be?"

Uh-oh. Joke, what joke indeed? I don't know any jokes! I'm a woman for God's sake, and women never remember jokes, right? Darn! A joke, a joke, I need a joke . . .

"Or is it one of those female jokes that might embarrass me, miss?"

"Yes, James, that's exactly it. It would embarrass both of us I'm afraid." Though, if I'd chosen the pee-in-my-pants option, James, I'm quite sure it would have been even more embarrassing for both of us.

My narrow escape from having to come up with a joke sobered me completely, and I was quite giggle-less by the time we arrived at the restaurant. The driver handed me off to the doorman who handed me off to the maitre d' who "had been expecting" me. He led me to a table tucked into an intimate corner. The restaurant was very posh in an understated sort of way. In the glow of candlelight, the well-heeled diners looked like a beautiful, animated Renoir painting. Voices were hushed, accompanied by the soft strains of a classical string quartet. My chair was pulled out for me, my napkin snapped open and placed delicately on my lap. The maitre d' leaned down and murmured softly, "Mr. Waters has called and should arrive momentarily. In the meantime, he wondered if you would like a cosmopolitan."

"Yes" I murmured back, "that would be delightful." I had absolutely no idea what a cosmopolitan was, but I hoped it was something to eat or drink. I had been so nervous all, day, I hadn't eaten at all, and I was famished.

A cosmopolitan, it turns out, is a beautiful red concoction that shows up in an extremely tippable martini glass. I don't know if it's traditional, but this one was filled to the absolute brim as if to test the law of surface tension. The waiter hovered over my shoulder, finally murmuring, "Would you like to taste it, miss, to see if it's to your satisfaction?"

Uh-oh. Could I ask for a sipper cup? Okay, Angie

Hawkins. You are out on a date in a fabulous restaurant. You arrived at this restaurant in a car driven by a man who wears a cap—a chauffeur's cap!—and you are surrounded by beautiful, sophisticated people. I stared sternly at the fragile-looking glass, daring it to spill, then carefully lifted it to my lips and took a very big sip.

"It's perfect," I murmured. Tah dah! I didn't spill a drop. When the waiter turned to leave, I took another swig to congratulate myself.

A cosmopolitan, besides being beautiful and served in a very tippable glass, is also quite strong. I felt the fiery liquid traveling down through my empty tummy. It was not a bad feeling at all. I took another big sip to see if the fiery feeling would continue. Yep, it did.

On my fourth sip, I looked up to see Ben coming toward me. He looked even more handsome than I had remembered. He was also looking very harried, though he grinned widely when he saw me.

"Angie! I'm so glad you got here safely! What a bum I am to be late. Please forgive me."

"Oh, I suppose I could." I smiled my flirty smile, the one I had practiced while brushing my teeth (I'm sure it looked better without the Colgate foam.).

"Good." Ben smiled back at me. "And you must be hungry. Shall I order for us?"

Shall he order for us? I had stumbled into a parallel universe, a utopia created specifically to please the females of our species. Where men dressed nicely, apologized for being late, and ordered food for us. Where drivers in caps—chauffeurs' caps!—picked us up and maitre d's expected us in their beautifully appointed restaurants. It brought to mind my last dinner date with Bob. We ordered with the motor running and seat belts fastened, wondering whether we were hungry enough to "Super Size It." Oh, Clarisse, if Ben is any indication of what else is out there, you are welcome to that sorry specimen!

"That would be nice," I murmured, having determined that murmuring was the appropriate tone in this universe.

Ben looked over the menu, conferred with the waiter, glancing at me occasionally for approval. I approved of everything, mainly because nothing that he suggested was in English and I had no idea what it might be. But I would have gladly eaten slugs, well-prepared ones of course, if that were the price to pay for this royal pampering.

"Angie, I haven't even paused to tell you how extraordinary you look this evening."

"Well, thank you, Ben."

"So who are you, Angie Hawkins? Tell me about yourself. I want to know everything."

Déjà vu? Wasn't that exactly how he had started our last conversation? But I guess our forty-five-minute exchange about fireflies and first touchdowns had left us both missing some critical data about one another. Besides, Ben was looking a little anxious and was probably just as nervous as I was. He is so suave and urbane that his nervousness made him a little more human.

"Well, I always start by bragging about my children."

"What are their names again?"

"Jenna and Tyler."

"Jenna and Tyler. Nice. Do you have a picture of them?"

Being the mother of the most beautiful children on earth, I am forced by law to carry several photos of them in my regular purse, but I could only fit one in my slim evening bag. This photo had been taken last summer. Tyler was home on break and he, Jenna, and I had driven to Santa Cruz. We were walking along the beach and had asked a passing tourist to take a picture of us. It turned out that the stranger's grasp of English and skill with cameras was minimal. He took several shots of our feet before he got one that that included all of our heads, but it was one of my all-time favorites: the three of us looked wind-blown, sunburned, and very happy to be together.

Ben held the photo close to the candle and studied it for a few moments. He reached across and touched my hand, a touch that made the fiery sensation of the cosmopolitan seem tepid in comparison.

"Angie, I can't believe you're old enough to be the mother of these children! You must have been a child bride!"

Even I, naïve as I am, know blarney when I hear it. But this was very sweet blarney, and his warm touch on my hand felt even sweeter. I kept my hand in that same place for the majority of the evening, just in case he decided to touch it again.

We continued to talk mainly about me, which I found highly unusual. Aren't most men better talkers than listeners? My evening "conversations" with Bob used to go something like this:

"So how was your day, Angie?"

"Well, I ran into some serious problems with . . ."

"That's good. Is dinner ready? I had a killer day, and you wouldn't believe yada yada yada."

I don't think men are just naturally lacking in curiosity. Most of them conscientiously research every single detail pertaining to their favorite sports hero, his batting average in Little League, when he was first traded and for how much, what product he uses for jock itch. But when it comes to their spouses and girlfriends, I think these same men would flunk even the short quiz.

But Ben was different. He wanted to know all about me and continued with his gentle probing. He made me feel completely at ease. In fact so much so that I started revealing some of the more gruesome aspects of my divorce, which according to *The Rules* is completely taboo. But I felt safe with Ben.

"I'm sorry it was so difficult for you, Angie." Ben's blue eyes were soft and sympathetic. "But it sounds as if you were fortunate to get out of a brain-numbing marriage. Some people don't get off that easily." It sounded as if there might be a very sad, personal story behind that comment. But Ben offered nothing further, so I didn't ask.

Toward dessert, I tried to turn the conversation to him. "So Ben, tell me about your work."

"Well, Angie, don't believe what you read or hear about me in the media. They make it sound as if my 'connections' have brought me all of my success. But that's simply not true. I'm just good at what I do."

Media? Connections? Uh-oh. Was I on a first date with a known celebrity? Known, that is, to everyone but me. See, unfortunately, or fortunately depending on your perspective, I have very little relationship with The Media. I don't read the newspaper, and I don't own a television. And someday, if the Committee for Un-American Activities is ever resurrected, I'm sure I'll be called before it.

"So, Mrs. Hawkins, it has been reported that you watch no

television, and in fact don't even own one. Can you explain yourself?"

"I believe, sir, that it is a matter of inefficiency."

"Inefficiency?"

"Yes. I used to watch television regularly. But ever since my children were born, I can't find enough time anymore. I seem to have misplaced my television-watching hours."

The senator shuffles through some notes and looks pointedly at the defendant. *"May I remind you, Mrs. Hawkins, that your children have not lived at home for several years."*

"Yes, well, I never relocated those missing hours. My day is totally full doing other things."

"How is it that 290 million Good Americans can find an average of three hours and forty-six minutes a day to watch television, and you cannot find any time at all?"

"Um, inefficiency?" The defendant squirms. The senator looks meaningfully at other committee members.

"Are you insinuating, Mrs. Hawkins, that there are no TV programs worth watching, worth making the time for?"

"Yes. I mean, no. I've been told about some really good programs, and I would watch them, but I'm somewhat disorganized. Whenever I turn on the TV, all I can find are reruns of Three's Company *or* Wide World of Bowling.*"*

"The record shall reflect that further investigation may be required on Mrs. Hawkins's attitudes regarding bowling."

"But I know about television! I know how survivors are voted off the island and who shot JR and . . ."

"Mrs. Hawkins, this committee is not interested in your secondhand knowledge. Now please explain to the committee why, additionally, you refuse to watch television news or purchase the local newspaper."

The defendant straightens defiantly in her seat. "Because, sir, that is not news."

"No? Then what would it be exactly?

"Voyeurism and mass media packaging."

"Voyeurism?"

"Yes. People and events being exploited as if each news story is an episode of As the World Turns.*"*

"I see. And packaging?"

"Yes, flashy titles rather than good reporting. 'Crisis in the White House,' 'America Under Siege: Day Two.' I want real news! I want Edward R. Murrow!" The defendant is led screaming out of the committee room, never to be seen again.

The upshot of this is that I had absolutely no idea what Ben was talking about nor what The Media had to say about him. Boycotting the news can make me feel smug and superior, but it can also make me feel pretty ignorant on occasion and this was definitely one of those occasions. I was too embarrassed to do anything more than smile and nod knowingly. I wasn't sure what I was supposed to know about Ben that only *I* didn't know versus what I didn't know that no one else knew either. So I couldn't figure out what questions I could or could not ask. Could I call my lifeline? As soon as Gwen or Jessica or Marie got home, I would ask them to fill me in.

Fortunately, the conversation was at a stopping point anyway. Dinner was over.

"Shall we go?"

We stood up from the table, me feeling a little woozy. That cosmopolitan on my empty stomach would have been enough. But Ben also ordered special wines; how could I say no? Every time I took the tiniest sip, Ben, gracious host that he is, made sure my glass was full again. By the time we walked out of the restaurant, I was rocking and rolling to ocean waves that didn't exist. Fortunately, Ben put his arm around me firmly. I hoped that my sway against him felt sexy rather than soused.

His car, a beautiful silver Lexus sports coupe, was magically waiting for us at the curb. I melted into the lovely leather seat, a tipsy Cinderella on her way home from the ball. Ben reached across me and buckled my seat belt, pausing on his way back to give me a sweet, soft kiss on the mouth. A considerate gentleman who wears seat belts and is a good kisser, who needed anything else?

Ben didn't ask for directions as he drove toward my place. I guess when you are a celebrity, or whatever he is, you have someone who figures these things out for you in advance. (*Miss Jones, my date this evening lives at 3626 Timbers Drive. Could you please give me directions from the La Papillion?*). He put in a CD, soft jazz guitar music, and we spoke very little as he drove. Everything was delightful, his company, the music, the cozy heated seat. Had I found the perfect man? Or was there a whole herd of Bens out there, just waiting for women like me?

Chapter 23

When we arrived, Ben stopped the car and looked at me shyly. "Angie, I can't tell you what a wonderful time I've had this evening." He placed his hand under my chin and kissed me, softly at first, then with more intensity. Now, did I happen to mention that I won first place in a kissing contest in the seventh grade? Decades might have passed, but critical survival skills (cramming for exams, kissing on a first date, and Pig Latin) never disappear completely. Here's my personal recipe for a really good kiss: start with your body just a little tense then *melt slowly* as the kiss progresses. Works every time. By the time Ben and I decided to go in, we had completely fogged up the windows of his car, the sign of a truly great makeout session.

Spud and Alli leaped to the door with an enthusiastic welcome. This quickly deteriorated as Spud, having determined that Ben was the mailman in disguise, started barking ferociously, all twenty pounds of Warrior beagle ready to attack. Soon Alli joined in the fray in a show of support, an International Union of Beagles imperative.

"I'm so sorry. They never do this. They must be getting overly protective having me all to themselves." I dragged the two unruly mutts into the bathroom and closed the door, leaving rawhide bones behind to quiet them.

"Shall I make us some coffee?" I was really nervous again. Looking around my little studio, the object that loomed most prominently was my B-E-D, with its mountain of Universal Womb pillows and freshly ironed sheets. Would we? *Should* we? My conscience held a debate with itself while my brain struggled with the intricacies of making coffee. Is it water, then coffee, or vice versa?

"Thanks, Angie, I'd like that. Shall I choose some music for us?" Ben had located the CD player, which was by the B-E-D, and was sorting through my new CDs. He chose a Diana Krall, very mellow, very romantic, very S-E-X-Y. Okay, I'm pretty sure you put the coffee in the little paper thing and the water . . .

Ben came up behind me in the kitchen, and I felt his breath at my ear. He brushed aside my hair, kissed the back of my neck, and, well, that was that. Uncertainty about what might happen next disappeared completely, and I abandoned all pretense of coffee making. My ambivalent conscience went on vacation to Venezuela, and the sutras of my kama took control. All I knew was that it felt wonderful to be kissed and held and fondled and . . .

Without going into that locker room detail men seem so fond of, suffice it to say that my mountain of pillows ended up on the floor along with all of our clothes, and Ben did get the pleasure of experiencing my newly ironed sheets. Somewhere in the midst of the kissing and stroking and bodies connecting, Ben pulled out a small metallic package. He was totally pocketless by then, so I have no idea where he pulled it from. "Angie, do you mind if I . . ." and with one hand, Ben unwrapped the condom and put it on while his other hand continued the moves that made me quiver. Ack! I had completely forgotten the safe sex part! But Ben had remembered. Ben, who seemed to think of everything, take care of everything, take control of everything . . .

When it was over, sated and breathless, we lay quietly wrapped around each other. I immersed myself in the warmth and feel of his body and inhaled the male smell of him. Without a word, he drifted off to sleep and, after a few pleasant minutes of listening to the rhythm of his breathing, so did I.

At around two in the morning, I woke up bleary-eyed to find Ben half-dressed and searching through the pillows on the floor.

"Hi."

"Hey, Angie." He sounded uneasy and self-conscious. "I need to get going. Big day today. I was just hunting for my socks."

Oh. Okay, so we must have hit the embarrassing Morning After stage. In the good old days, we could pull out a cigarette and blow a few smoke rings to get through the awkwardness. Pity cigarettes turned out to be so carcinogenic. Why hadn't someone come up with a good post-coital substitute? Like tobacco-flavored lollipops? Yuck! Okay, maybe not that. How about bubble rings that blow smoke rather than bubbles? Ben continued to stumble through the pillows on the floor.

"Shall I turn on the light?"

"No, no. I don't want to disturb you. I'll find them." He rooted around for a few more moments while I watched him sleepily. "Here they are!" Stuffing them into his pocket, he sat down beside me on the bed. He pushed tousled hair back from my face, gazing at me silently. I closed my eyes and felt him kiss me gently on the forehead—probably to avoid my horrendous morning breath, but it was a nice gesture anyway.

"Dear little Angie, last night was wonderful. It will definitely go into my scrapbook of memories. I'll call you," and he was gone.

I curled up under the covers again. "My scrapbook of memories . . ." What a quaint and sweet thing to say! I drifted off to sleep again.

Chapter 24

Ben must have opened the bathroom door before he left (or Alli figured out how to turn the doorknob, which is highly possible if she thought there might be food on the other side) because the two pups had resumed their normal snuggle position with me in bed by the time I woke up. Amidst beagle smells, I could still smell Ben on my skin. How delicious! I had no early calls or appointments that Thursday morning, so I nuzzled back under the covers and mused over the prior evening.

The date? It was fantastic, a fairy-tale first date. Ben was charming and the conversation was delightful (at least until I hit the snag of not knowing that my date was some kind of celebrity). The food was scrumptious (whatever the heck it was), and the wine was wonderful (though next time, I'd be better off not sampling quite so much of it). I didn't trip, spill, or break anything, and my hair stayed poofed all evening. All in all, I'd give the date a 9.5.

The sex? Okay, honestly how had it been? Well, honestly? Just okay. I was nervous, and I know I rushed things once it was obvious where we were headed. We had "cut to the chase" before I was quite ready, though admittedly foreplay in this case had started the moment Ben showed up at the restaurant. I hadn't been able to relax fully and lose myself in the moment, though Ben hadn't seemed to notice or mind. Maybe I was just trying too hard to "drive my man wild." But more importantly, I was disappointed that we just fell asleep afterward. Talking after sex is often more intimate than the physical act itself; without it, something is really missing. I'd have to rate the sex a 6.0.

So all in all, how did I feel about the evening? Actually pretty good, very good in fact. Maybe because I finally felt released from being Bob's ex-wife. Maybe because I had felt desired by a very attractive man. Maybe because I had "felt the fear and did it anyway" and now knew that I could.

Were a string of One-Night-Stands in my future? Probably not. It was fun, but it lacked something, that closeness and "in love" feeling that makes sex so much, um, sexier for me. Would I like to see Ben again? Oh, yes. But honestly, as kind and sweet, gallant and attractive as he was, there was just something that didn't connect for me. Maybe I didn't know him well enough yet. Maybe I wanted to explore the other Bens that might be out there. Or maybe I just wasn't ready to find The One and get right back into picking up some guy's socks again and sharing toothpaste.

And that's when it hit me that I was enjoying living alone. Not that I need to stay this way forever, but there were certain freedoms in being by myself. Thinking only of what I want to eat, what I want to do. Staying up reading as late as I want to or taking naps in the middle of the afternoon. Deciding what to throw out and what to keep. Trying on new personalities and costumes. Yep, I think being unattached, with a few romantic encounters interspersed, is just what I want for the time being. "Live close by and visit often" just might become my motto for a while.

I got up, put on a pot of coffee (incredibly, this morning I had no trouble remembering how it was made). My place looked like it had been hit by a tornado, which in a sense it had. Pillows and clothes were scattered everywhere from the kitchen through the office to the bedroom. Okay, so that would make it only a ten-foot by ten-foot swath, but it was still a mess.

As I picked up each article of my abandoned clothing, I recalled in detail how it had been removed from my body to end up on the floor. Like viewing videos of past family celebrations, it wasn't quite as experiential as the actual event, but it brought back the sensations pretty clearly. Who knew tidying up could be such a turn-on?

The one item that remained missing was my fancy little thong, not surprising considering it's half the size of a Post-it note. The beagles had a penchant for stealing and hiding my underwear so I'd have to look later. In the meantime, I always had my "moment of truth" undies to wear if an emergency dating situation arose. Listen to me, going from "haven't dated in twenty-six years" to "might have an emergency date before the next load of laundry!"

I dressed and got on with my day, doing all of the normal things: errands, conference calls, e-mails to Phil. But all through the day, I just felt different. Sexier? More confident? Liberated from past ghosts? Were my chakras open and was my feminine power fully expressing itself? However you choose to define it, I just felt good and was eager to share my breakthrough with my trio of best friends. None of them would be home until Friday night, but I didn't want to call them. That should be a face-to-face kind of discussion. How impressed they would be that I, Angie Hawkins, had gone "all the way!"

Chapter 25

I went to the office on Thursday and Friday, but my afterglow brought on brain freeze. I had annual budgets to prepare for seventeen properties. I had memos to write outlining leasing strategies and an analysis of a purchase contract to develop. I had to summarize the performance of Phil's portfolio to date. Could I do any of that? No. If this witless daze was characteristic of my new chapter, I'd better find myself a job as a parking meter.

I was dying to tell someone about my date with Ben, but my best friends were still out of town. Lilah would have been interested, but I wasn't quite ready to discuss my romantic adventures with my mother-in-law. So I retold the story to myself, creating better descriptions, inserting appropriate dramatic pauses, capturing each romantic moment (still remaining discreet of course; a lady never tells all!). By late Friday afternoon, the story was getting pretty titillating and I was ready for my audience. Get home, get home, get home!

I sat at my desk, using my besotted brain to analyze

when Ben might phone and the odds of more Bens being out there, when Marie called.

"Angie, we're about to get on the plane, but we missed our first flight so I thought I'd let you know that we'll be home really late tonight. I didn't want you to worry."

Women do this for each other. If we're running late, we call. If we can't drive the carpool, we arrange for a substitute. If we might miss a deadline on that important project, we give you plenty of lead time and come up with a fallback plan.

"Okay, so Jack told me you had a date. Do NOT tell me about it because I'll want to hear every single detail, and there isn't time. But how was the rest of the Artists' reception? I saw you schmoozing with Beatrice Bennett's husband. Working some in-roads for Tyler?"

"Huh? What do you mean?"

"Don't you remember him? Ben. Ben Waters. You looked like you were almost flirting with the man, for gosh sakes! What a mother won't do to secure her son's future! But really, Angie, I doubt it will do much good. I've heard that his marriage with Judge Bennett is not great. She definitely wears the pants in the family. Jack thinks Ben is a lightweight, an ambulance chaser he calls him. But he's not bad-looking. Anyway, did you meet anyone interesting at the party?"

"Uh . . ."

"Oh, wait, they're starting to board. I've got to run. See you soon, Angie, and you can tell me all about the big date." Click.

Hummmmm. Bleep, bleep, bleep. *If you'd like to make a call, please hang up. Wait for the dial tone and . . .*

I replaced the receiver very carefully as if it might shatter. I moved my body from the desk very slowly, as if my body might shatter. I started thinking very cautiously as if my mind might shatter.

I felt betrayed. I thought there must be some mistake. I felt stupid. I thought about things Ben had said and hadn't said. I felt panicked. I thought about Tyler and his pending interview. My thoughts and emotions were all jumbled and crashing into each other. I grabbed us all and sat us down to get organized.

Okay. Ben Waters is married to Beatrice Bennett. Beatrice Bennett is Judge Bennett. Judge Bennett is the person who will be interviewing my son one week from today. So.

That means that I just slept with a married man. A married man who is married to Judge Bennett. Judge Bennett, who is a vicious, unforgiving bitch. So if Judge Bennett finds out that I slept with her husband, she will destroy my son's career.

Did Ben Waters tell me he was married? No. Did I ever ask him? No. Is that deception on his part or incredible naïveté on mine? I don't know. But Beatrice the Bitch will destroy my son's career anyway.

And that was the thought that finally propelled me into action, launching me from my seat to the Yellow Pages to look up Ben's office address. Perhaps I should have had enough anger on my own behalf to motivate me. But that nasty little gremlin who always tells me that I am unworthy/undeserving/unlovable had joined the clamor in my head and was stating its case. This ugly voice (a lifelong companion) would have paralyzed me completely. But with my baby boy in danger, I had to do something.

There it was: Ben Waters, Esq. Personal Injury. I grabbed my purse (even in a psychotic breakdown, a true woman always grabs her purse) and headed to the downtown address listed.

I tried to keep my whacked-out emotions and thoughts in some kind of order as I drove to Ben's office. Surely there was some reasonable explanation for all of this. Maybe Ben and Beatrice had secretly divorced and no one knew about it. Maybe this was a totally different Ben Waters, another Ben Waters Personal Injury attorney who had attended the Artists Guild benefit. Maybe I was in the middle of some bizarre nightmare and I would wake up to find my five-year-old Tyler, safely asleep in his Superman pajamas in his room down the hall.

And then I had one of those thunderbolt intuitions. My panties. The "special occasion" thong that had been missing since Ben and I had, um, removed it. I had looked in all of Spud's and Alli's usual hiding places but had never found it. Somehow I just knew that Ben had picked it up and stuffed it in his pocket on his way out that morning. How did I know? If you've got that extra X chromosome, then you know how I know. If you don't, ask your mother or your wife. I knew, that's all, I just knew.

Chapter 26

The trappings of Ben's office led me to believe that he had caught some pretty lucrative ambulances over the years. The receptionist looked up from a riveting examination of her brilliant red nails.

"May I help you?" Her tone seemed to add "though I'd rather not."

"I'm here to see Ben Waters. My name is Angie Hawkins. It's urgent."

"Do you have an appointment?" Of course I don't have an appointment, you twit! If he had told me a week ago that he was married to my son's future employer and was only coming on to me so he could have a quick fling and steal my undies, perhaps I would have had the foresight to make an appointment. But the jerk didn't so . . .

"No, I don't. But I'm certain he'll see me." Her look told me that she was certain he wouldn't. But she picked up the phone and mumbled something into it.

"Well, apparently he is willing to see you. Down the

hall, second door to the left." She pointed over her shoulder and went back to her nails.

My knees were a little wobbly as I walked down the hall. I was rattled, and my brain was not fully functioning. I hadn't had much time to think this through. What was it I had planned to say? I knocked twice and entered Ben's dark-wood-paneled office.

"Ben." Good start.

"Angie, what on earth are you doing here?" Bad start. He did not look pleased to see me and remained seated behind his oversized mahogany desk.

"Ben, um, I found out this afternoon that you are married . . ."

"Don't be ridiculous! You knew I was married. I told you who I was."

"Well, no, I actually didn't know you were married because you told me your name, but I didn't recognize it and didn't know who you were."

"You're kidding! You honestly hadn't ever heard of Ben Waters? I'm in the papers all the time. Attorney to the famous and infamous, married to the darling of the Republican party, Beatrice Bennett. And my TV segment on Channel 3? *You Too Can Sue?* Everybody knows who I am!" He looked incredulous. "Now this is really choice!" And Ben started to laugh. The laugh that had sounded so charming and boyish just two nights ago, sounded revolting. This interaction was not going in a positive direction. He paused and wiped the slimy mirth out of his deceitful eyes.

"Well, so what can I do for you? You're obviously beyond the age of getting pregnant from our little romp."

And he started laughing again, totally enthralled with his own cleverness. My stomach was getting queasy; my utter stupidity and lack of judgment flooded over me. What a disgusting jerk! How could I have possibly . . . ? But I had to pull myself together and stick to my mission.

"No, um, it's just that I need to make sure that your wife never finds out about it. And, well, I think you have something that belongs to me, and I want to get it back."

His eyes narrowed. Why hadn't I noticed before how obscenely piglike and sneaky those eyes were?

"And why would this be, little Angie? I'm sure you have other sexy little panties to wear. Are you a friend of Beatrice?" The creep propped his feet up on the desk, looking even more arrogant and disdainful.

"Oh, no, I've never met her. But see, my son Tyler just graduated from law school and he will be coming into town next week to interview with her for a clerk position. If Judge Bennett ever found out that Tyler's mother had, well, been with her husband . . . It's just that I've heard that your wife can be, uh, kind of . . ."

"Vindictive? Cruel? Unreasonable? Yes, I'd say that's pretty accurate." He looked at me with no sympathy at all, then stared up at the ceiling as if in thought. I racked my mind for something to say, some argument that would persuade Ben to act like the decent human being that he obviously wasn't. But my brain had gone into overwhelm and was whimpering in the corner of my skull: *Poor Tyler! Poor Angie! Poor Tyler! Poor Angie!*

Finally, Ben grinned to himself, brought his feet down from the desk and stood up. "Okay, Angie, I'm going to show you something and let you in on a little secret. I've wanted to share this with someone and haven't been able to. So I guess you've given me the opportunity." He went to the bookcase and pulled down a large thick portfolio.

"Now to make a very long story short, I've been trying to get a divorce from my wife, Beatrice the Bitch as she is known, for many years now. But, as you are apparently aware, Beatrice is an ogre, ogress actually. And to support her very grand ambitions, she is determined to have her party view her as a beacon of family values, successful and successfully married."

Ben pulled some keys from his pocket and worked the tiny lock on the side of the portfolio. It reminded me of the tiny locks on my glossy pink Dear Diaries. Somehow, I doubted that this one protected Ben's innocent descriptions of adolescent crushes and first kisses.

"So, um, so why don't you just leave her?"

"Oh, no, little Angie." I hated that "little Angie" thing; it was so patronizing and smarmy! "I couldn't do that because Beatrice would see to it that I was ruined completely. She's fully capable of that, you know."

The little diary lock popped open but Ben left the book closed to continue his lecture. "But I came up with a plan, and our governor is giving me the opportunity I need. See, in the first days of November, he'll announce dear Beatrice as his appointee to the California Supreme Court. Now, as a new, supposedly brilliant and conservative appointee, who by the way must be ratified in general election within one year, what do you think might be more embarrassing, more damaging than being divorced?"

Think, think! My brain was of no use, still off somewhere whimpering pathetically: *Poor Tyler! Poor Angie!*

"No guesses? I'll tell you what would be worse. Being married to a man who has been systematically having affairs right under your nose!" And with that, Ben snapped the lock and flipped open the portfolio with a flourish.

At first, I couldn't quite figure out what I was looking at. It looked like a butterfly collection, only with pretty bits of lace pinned flat rather than insects, photos and handwritten dates and descriptions beneath. Oh my God! This was a scrapbook of Ben's conquests, each one memorialized by a pair of panties, like a scalp collection. He flipped through the pages. Pink bikini, blue thong, pictures of young women, others my age. My stomach was seriously queasy now. And there, #13, was my black lace thong and the picture of Tyler, Jenna, and me taken at the beach last summer. I started to shake.

"See, Angie, it's foolproof!" Ben was talking faster now, obviously excited to be able to share his genius with someone. "I'll show this to Beatrice an hour before he's scheduled to announce her appointment. That way, she won't have any time to think. She either gives me a divorce, with a hefty settlement, or I take this story, scrapbook and all, to *People* magazine and get paid a bundle for the exclusive story. Either way I win."

And either way, I lose. Come on, brain! Pull it together!

"Yes, well, Ben, it does seem to be a very, uh, clever scheme. And I'm sure it will work. But do you suppose you could, uh, just leave me out of it? Just give me my stuff back? You seem to have plenty of other, uh, material." I felt guilty about not trying to save Ben's other victims, but with my brain on sabbatical and my legs barely able to support me, I didn't think I had the strength.

"Well, Angie, I was just thinking about that." Glimmer of hope! "But I decided against it." Scrapbook slammed shut, hope crushed. "See, I think by having you in there with your son, someone she will have just met, it's going to feel that much more real to her. Like I could be having sex with anyone around her, invading her space. Sorry about that."

"But, but . . ." My brain had shut down completely, not even a whimper left.

"Now, why don't you go home, little Angie." Ben took my elbow and steered me toward the door. "And tell your son that Mom has been very naughty and he may want to start applying for other jobs." We were at the door. He turned the doorknob, his other hand still on my elbow, his breath on my neck. "And you know. Angie," he whispered in my ear. "I enjoyed our night together. If you ever feel like repeating it, you just give me a call."

I turned toward him. And then I made the most naturally eloquent gesture I've ever made in my life: I barfed all over him.

Chapter 27

I don't remember walking out of Ben's office, going down the elevator, going to my car in the parking lot. I don't remember driving home and parking the car. I don't remember unlocking my front door and entering the house. I don't remember going into my kitchen, putting my purse down, or walking into the shower and turning the water on full force. But I must have done all of those things because I found myself standing there under the streaming water, clothes, shoes, and all. And then I started to cry.

I cried for my total humiliation and for the disaster that was about to befall Tyler because of me. I cried because I hadn't known there were such ugly, nasty, despicable people in the world and because I had chosen this ugly, nasty, despicable person for my first date in thirty years. I cried because I felt hopeless and helpless and didn't know what I had done to deserve all of this.

I finally turned off the shower, stripped off my soggy clothes, and left them on the shower floor. I toweled off and put on my bathrobe and climbed into bed. Spud and Alli leaped in beside me, snuggling their beagle bodies close to mine, big brown eyes looking at me with concern. And I started to cry again.

I've always had this theory that modern women don't cry enough. We're all so busy keeping our lives going, being strong, coping. There just aren't enough convenient moments in our lives to fall apart and thoroughly weep. But hadn't I already caught up on my crying quota during the miserable eighteen months after my divorce? Apparently not.

As it grew darker outside, Spud and Alli nudged me to be fed. I dragged my body out of bed, my mind feeling dead and numb, and stumbled to the kitchen. Maybe this was it. Maybe I would just live the rest of my ruined life like some surburban zombie, feeding the dogs, going to work, sleeping.

Or maybe I wouldn't do anything at all. Just lie there until it was all over. Marie would find the dogs howling over my dead body and she would take care of them. Tyler would know that his mother was so pitifully sorry for what she had done to him that she just laid down and died. Isn't that what they did in those old folk ballads? They "jist laid themselves down and died?" I crawled back into bed and arranged myself in coffin-ready position, arms crossed over my chest, legs straight and together. Then I wept again until my pillow was soaked.

Finally I was cried out, I fell into a fitful half-sleep dreaming dreams as desolate as my new reality. But around midnight I woke with a start. Something was wrong. My bed didn't feel like the safe haven it usually is for me.

"It's the sheets," a voice inside me whispered. Ack! my sheets! I could still detect the faint smell of Ben in them.

"Damn, damn, damn!" Startling the pups, I leaped out of bed and ripped off the offending linens. "How will I ever get rid of the revolting, disgusting, slimey, obnoxious, putrid smell?"

"Sulfuric acid? Or why don't you burn them? Exorcise the demon's presence."

"Three hundred dollar sheets? I don't think so! I wouldn't give him the satisfaction!"

I continued fuming and sputtering, while I remade the bed with clean, untainted linens. Wait! Maybe that wasn't enough. What if some of his dead skin cells had sloughed off onto the mattress? To make doubly sure, I stripped off the new sheets, flipped over the mattress, and remade the bed all over again. When I finally sat down, puffing from the exertion, I felt better, almost alive.

"All right, Angie Hawkins," I told myself sternly. "It's time to get a grip. It's not like I haven't done stupid things before."

Not this stupid.

"And I've been in lots of other sticky situations."

"This one is to 'sticky' what Super Glue is to Elmer's."

"And I've always come out on top."

"I believe you were 'on top' when Ben was stinking up your sheets."

"I can fix this. I know I can. Where there's a will, there's a way."

"You have no will left and there's no way out of this one."

191

"Will you shut up? This is ridiculous! I'm arguing with myself and I'm losing!"

I'm just trying to be realistic.

"Well, you're not helping, all right?" I know it's psychologically questionable to talk to yourself like this, especially when yourself is talking back to you rudely. But I wasn't really the epitome of sanity just then. I stomped into the kitchen to make myself a peanut butter and jelly sandwich and a glass of milk, the Universal Comfort Food. I sat at the kitchen table and tried to sort through the whole situation, starting from the beginning.

"Okay, so how on earth did I get myself into this mess in the first place?"

"Well, you didn't get yourself into it totally by yourself. You had a little help."

To heck with sanity; the conversation was becoming interesting. "What do you mean 'help'?"

"Well, as I recall, you got quite a bit of encouragement from your three best friends."

"That's absolutely right! If they hadn't talked me into unleashing Tantric juices and expanding horizons, I wouldn't be in this mess at all! It's completely and totally their fault!"

"Well, perhaps not totally . . ."

"Oh, put a sock in it!"

Now I was mad, which I think is a positive sign in the evolution of a psychotic breakdown, don't you? I grabbed the phone and punched in three different phone numbers, getting three different voice mail boxes, but leaving the very same message on all three:

"This is Angie and I need you to be at my house tomorrow morning by 9:00 A.M. sharp. This is an emergency."

I slammed down the receiver after the last message, It was 4:00 A.M. by the time I finally flopped into bed to sleep the deep sleep of the righteously indignant.

Chapter 28

My three so-called best friends arrived at my place precisely at nine o'clock. I'm sure none of us could remember when we'd all been together last, especially in a place as small as my little studio. They greeted one another courteously, if somewhat dubiously, and stood looking at me impatiently.

Gwen spoke first. "So, Angie, what is this all about?"

"Have a seat." My tone was not courteous, nor dubious. I was Charlton Heston ready to read the riot act to those wayward Israelites. Gwen and Jessica sat at the kitchen table, while Marie settled in my office chair. I sat on the bed, which meant that we were all within thirty-seven inches of each other.

"The three of you have ruined my life completely and irrevocably." My dramatic delivery was stirring, but so far my audience was only stirred to mild curiosity. I continued.

"Following your ill-advised guidance, I entered into a brief illicit relationship with a married man, who is using mementos of the affair to blackmail his wife and, in doing so, ruin my son's future legal career!" I had planned to pound the table for emphasis, but due to the unfortunate seating arrangement, had to thump on a throw pillow instead.

"Angie, what are you talking about?" Jess's tone of annoyed confusion was mirrored on Marie's and Gwen's faces. "Could you skip the theatrics and just explain what kind of trouble you've gotten yourself into?"

"I didn't get myself into trouble! You three got me into this! You told me I should have a One Night Stand, open up my chakras, regain my feminine power, broaden my horizons!"

Jessica looked at me incredulously. "Well, I certainly don't recall suggesting you get involved with a married man! Gwen? Marie? I can't say I know you two that well, but I can't imagine you giving her that advice either." They shook their heads emphatically, clearly appalled at the mere suggestion. "So, why would you do such a thing, Angie? It just doesn't seem like you."

"But I didn't know he was married!" My righteous indignation was wavering; my tone disintegrated from Charlton Heston to Pee Wee Herman. "He wasn't wearing a wedding ring!"

"He wasn't wearing a wedding ring." Gwen paused with a heavy sigh, a prayer really: *Dear God, help me be patient with the world of idiots that surrounds me.* "Angie, many married men do not wear wedding rings. The presence of a ring says something. The absence of one does not." She turned to the other two for agreement and got it.

"Okay, Angie." Marie spoke calmly to ward off my rising hysteria. "Just start from the beginning. What exactly happened?"

"Well, I was at that Artists Guild reception. I met Ben Waters, and we hit it off and . . ."

"You got it on with Beatrice the Bitch's husband? Are you *crazy?*" Gwen's unflappability had completely flapped.

"But I didn't know that . . ."

"You didn't know who Ben Waters is?!? Everyone knows who he is!" Jessica's voice exceeded all prior levels of shrill. "He and his wife have their pictures in the newspaper all the time for some charity event or other. Especially now that she might run for office."

"And Ben does that legal spot on Channel 3 every Thursday night. Jack says he's a smarmy ambulance chaser, but I guess he's photogenic. Angie, how could you have possibly missed . . ." And there Marie's voice trailed off as it dawned on her and the others at the same time. Angie does not watch television. Angie does not read the newspaper. Angie is totally clueless. We observed a solemn silence as the three of them tried to fathom the depth of my ignorance.

Finally, Gwen spoke as if they had been thinking aloud together. "Well, she does listen to NPR."

"So she probably does know about Afghanistan." Jessica is always looking for the positive.

"But knows nothing about local news in Sacramento." Marie is very pragmatic. She sighed. "Okay, Angie. Take it from the top."

So I told them the whole story: the Pinot Grigio, his purple Hermès tie, our romantic dinner that ended up at my place ("Did you at least use a condom?" Probably the only thing I had done right.), my missing panties, and the final barfing scene at Ben's office (Okay, so maybe the second thing I had done right.).

"So, see, I'm really in trouble here. When Judge Bennett finds out that Tyler's mother is lucky #13 in Ben's scrapbook, I'm sure she won't hire him, and he'll be crushed."

"Oh, I'd bet she'll do more than that," Gwen broke in grimly. "That woman was a horrible vindictive bitch when I knew her in college, and she's gotten worse as she's aged. I wouldn't put it past her to see that Tyler gets blackballed completely."

"Oh, God!" I moaned and flopped back hopelessly into my mountain of pillows, burying my face. There was another very long silence. Marie was first to recover.

"Well, all right. I guess as her closest friends and having had years of experience with Angie, we should have kept in mind how naïve she can be. Perhaps we should have been a little more cautious in encouraging her to branch out into new social adventures. Not that we are to blame for all this . . ."

"No, but you have a point there," Gwen agreed. "I remember even from our college days, you had to give her very specific instructions, or she would run amok. Like the bra-burning ceremony our freshman year. She thought she had to keep the bra on while it was burned, and showed up with all kinds of ointments and bandages . . ."

"Oh, and she gets totally gung ho when she starts anything," Jess chimed in. "I remember our birthing class when she got so overzealous with the breathing exercises that she passed out. The instructor said she'd never seen anyone do that before."

"And her judgment on the subject of men has always

been horrible. She married Bob, for God's sake!" Marie added.

The three of them continued discussing my foibles and faults freely and enthusiastically, as if I wasn't even in the room. They had decades of material to cover. I buried myself deeper into my pillows, running through thoughts of the "worst thing that could happen." It's an exercise that my mother taught me as a child. When everything looks bleak, you just think about the absolutely worst thing that could result from this situation and usually even the absolutely worst result isn't impossible to survive. But my worsts just kept getting more and more dismal. Tyler blackballed from the entire legal community. The only job he can find is at In-'N-Out Burger, and he never speaks to me again. He moves with his future children, my grandchildren, across the country so they will never be exposed to their evil grandmother, the floozy who ruined their daddy's life . . . I was yanked out of my suicide-inspiring reverie by a single word: flipchart.

"Huh?" I shifted a pillow so that my miserable face was just barely exposed.

"Angie, do you have . . . no, wait! I've still got mine in the car." Jessica ran out the door with her car keys.

"What do we need a flipchart for?"

"So we can brainstorm and come up with a plan to get you out of this mess, of course." Gwen didn't add "Duh!" but it was obviously in her voice.

"You . . . you really think we can do something about this? But Ben was so awful, and his wife is so mean and . . ."

"Angie"—Marie pulled me up to a sitting position—

"don't be such an impossibility thinker! You have three very smart, dynamic, and resourceful best friends. Let us see what we can come up with."

Jessica wrestled her flipchart and easel through the front door. We rearranged furniture, moving the kitchen table into the office (in other words, eighteen inches to the left), and positioned the chart so we could all see it.

"All right." Jessica uncapped a big black marker. "I recommend we start with a charter, a statement of purpose. Shall we call this the *Save Angie* project for now?" There was murmured agreement, and she wrote SAVE ANGIE in big block letters across the top of the page.

I had never witnessed Jessica in her professional capacity as a facilitator, but she was really quite good, asking questions, drawing out thoughts, distilling them down into a few words. Gwen and Marie participated adeptly, and the three of them worked in well-ordered harmony. Maybe it was their basic professionalism, or the urgency of my predicament, or the bond they formed while reminiscing about my deficiencies (which they had agreed to be numerous), but their long-standing animosity toward one another was nowhere to be seen. As for me, I was a pretty weak contributor thanks to lack of sleep and overwrought emotions. Fortunately the team didn't expect much of me. Within ten minutes, we had our *Save Angie* charter:

Project Background: Ben Waters, desiring a divorce from his wife, has embarked on a scheme of blackmail that involves revealing the catalogue of his promiscuous adventures to his wife, Judge Bennett. Angie has, by her actions, earned a place in this catalogue. Tyler will be interviewing with Judge Bennett for employment. The inclusion of his mother in the aforementioned catalogue will not be viewed positively by his potential employer.

Project Goal: To ensure that Judge Bennett does not view the evidence of Angie's inappropriate interaction with Ben Waters thereby removing any barriers to Tyler's future legal career that are directly caused by his mother's wanton act.

Scope: Reclaim and/or destroy the evidence, specifically Angie's Special Occasion Panties.

Not in the Scope of this Project: Provide guarantee that Tyler will get hired. Instigate appropriate punishment for Ben Waters's crimes against womanhood. Damage control for any of Angie's future wanton acts.

"Couldn't we change 'wanton' to 'ill-advised'? I'm not feeling particularly wanton, just incredibly stupid."

"How about 'indiscretion'?" Gwen offered. "It avoids any assumption of culpability or specific intent." It's always good to have an attorney in the room.

"Okay, so let's move on to the team members for this project and their skill sets." Jessica pulled out a green marker. "As far as I know, there are four of us." She wrote GWEN, MARIE, JESSICA, and ANGIE on a new page, leaving room beneath each name. "Anyone else?"

"Well, I'm sure Jack would be willing to help."

"Oh, no, Marie!" I popped up from the pillow coffin I had built over myself. "You can't tell Jack about any of this!"

"But I tell Jack everything. He's very trustworthy."

"I know he is, Marie, but this is so humiliating." I was certain that even Spud and Alli thought less of me these days.

"Okay, Angie, but I'm sure he could be useful."

"What about Jenna? Talk about a resourceful young woman!" Jessica and Marie nodded their agreement. I merely groaned and reburied myself.

"Okay, so no Jenna. I guess it's just the four of us. So now let's write down any of our personal or professional talents, skills or attributes that could be useful for this project. Gwen? Why don't you start?"

"Okay, well, I've known Beatrice the Bitch for years. I wouldn't say we're intimate, but I can read her pretty well. And let's see, obviously, I am a legal resource if Angie ends up getting sued as a home wrecker." My muffled groan was barely audible through the pillows. Gwen's list continued: research capabilities (Internet, private detectives) composition of intimidating letters, race-car-driving skills with an SCCA license including training in kidnap avoidance techniques ("Really? How interesting! Could you show us sometime?").

"And I own a handgun, a Colt 45. I'm a fairly skilled markswoman."

"What?" I came back to life. "Gwen, we absolutely, positively have no use whatsoever for a gun! We're certainly not going to hold somebody up or kill anyone for gosh sakes!"

Three sets of eyes turned and stared me down. I was obviously out of sync with the team on this one.

"Angie," Jess remonstrated sternly, "we are brainstorming. During the brainstorming phase of planning, there are no bad or unacceptable ideas." She wrote "45 and can use it" in big clear print on Gwen's list.

The lists expanded. Among other things, Jessica's included: expertise in project planning and logistics, rock and tree climbing, and knowledge of herbal recipes for psychedelics and sleep potions ("We're not planning to drug anyone!" "Angie, please don't disrupt our flow here."). Marie's skill in origami didn't make the list (though we did take a fifteen-minute break so she could show us how to make small and large cranes out of typing paper). But she had an extensive Who's Who database for Sacramento, a degree in psychology with a minor in criminal law ("I am especially good at psychoanalysis of serial killers."), and a brown belt in tae kwon do. Additionally, it was unanimously agreed that Marie's extraordinary gift for attracting the opposite sex could be quite useful.

All three asset lists were pretty full: and then it came to mine. The ANGIE list was blank so far. I didn't move from under my safe little pillow world, but listened very attentively.

"So, Angie. Hmmm. Let's see." There was a very long pause, three geniuses momentarily stumped. "Ah! Well, she's got a minivan!"

"Yes! Good, write that down. A minivan could be very helpful." Another long pause. Even I tried to think of what I could contribute. But the only qualities I came up with were the very ones that had gotten me into this mess in the first place.

"Wait! What about this?" Marie was excited. "She's definitely got a high level of motivation to see that this project succeeds. An extraordinary level of motivation, wouldn't you say?"

"Yes! It's that maternal protectiveness instinct, mother lion protecting her cub!" Gwen sounded excited, too. "With that level of motivation, she'll have enough adrenaline flowing to do just about anything. Like lift up cars or throw herself in front of buses!"

"Good thinking, team! And she's so completely humiliated at this point, that she'd probably be willing to do anything, like, say, run naked through the mall to create a diversion. What has she got to lose?" Jessica wrote EXTREMELY MOTIVATED, WILL DO THE EXTRAORDINARY.

Oh, goody. Just when I thought it couldn't get any worse, it could. I would soon be jumping off tall buildings and flashing in public. But here in my lovely, lovely pillow world, it was still safe. I tried to will myself into a coma.

Through the brainstorming session I dozed off and on, exhausted and depressed. Jack showed up around noon with sandwiches, which made him instantly popular with the team. But he was shooed out the door after quick introductions.

We had progressed through Resources and Potential Broad Strategies. The Broad Strategies list included, but was not limited to: *Burn Down Their House. Kill Ben. Kill Beatrice. Create a Diversionary Disaster to Derail the Candidacy Announcement (Killing Spree, Major Traffic Accident, etc.).* It is interesting to note that not one of these options was discarded based on criteria of moral standards or prison term anticipated. Rather, they were dropped because they did not guarantee the required results. The only strategy that seemed to accomplish the goal fully was *Steal Back the Incriminating Articles*. In light of the other potential strategies, this one sounded quite reasonable.

Next we tackled time frames and deadlines. From what Ben had told me, he planned to reveal the contents of his scrapbook and make his demands of Beatrice on the day the governor announces her appointment. By our calculations, that would be either on Sunday, November 2 (Sunday being the favored day for family values politicians to make statements) or early Monday, November 3. Tyler's interview with Judge Bennett was on the Friday a few days before, which was Halloween.

Marie sat up straight in her chair, her face excited. "Hey, wait a minute! Doesn't the Legal Aid Society put on some kind of Halloween night fund-raiser?"

"Yes, I think so. It usually draws a huge crowd. Everybody in town shows up. Why?" Gwen was wrestling with her latest paper crane, its little wings somehow crisscrossed over its tail.

"Because I think it's being hosted this year at the home of Beatrice Bennett and Ben Waters! Jack and I had thought about going, but he is opening up the railroad display to kids that night. I'm sure there are still tickets available."

The rest of the team seemed pretty enthusiastic about the event. But personally, I wasn't thrilled to go to a party thrown by the couple who were about to ruin Tyler's life and, therefore, mine. And I said so, only to elicit those exasperated *Oh, Angie!* looks that were becoming so common lately.

"Angie!" Jessica was practically jumping up and down at her easel. "Pay attention! If he is showing the scrapbook to Beatrice on Sunday or first thing Monday, he's probably doing it at their home. And if he is, odds are he'll bring it home with him Friday rather than drive all the way back to the office over the weekend to get it. Ergo, the scrapbook will be somewhere in their house on Friday evening during the party!"

Oh. Well, "ergo" might be stretching it a bit, but I could follow her logic.

"I've been there! I've been in that house! I'll bet I can draw a layout of the place." Gwen ditched her lame crane and grabbed a marker. "The place is huge and . . ."

From that point, plans for the caper (the team had agreed that a burglary on Halloween definitely rated caper status) fell together quickly. General Schwarzkopf might have found it a little sketchy, but here was the basic strategy:

A) Gwen would distract Beatrice, ensuring that she stayed occupied during the party so that B) Marie could put the moves on Ben and seduce him into showing her the scrapbook whereupon C) she would tell me where the scrapbook was stashed, and I would swipe it and D) hand it to Jessica, who would be positioned somewhere outside ready to receive the scrapbook and spirit it away. Maybe I was too brain-dead from emotional stress and lack of sleep, but it was all beginning to sound, well, almost plausible.

"So, now, we need to go out and get our costumes!" Even Gwen was acting like a little kid, eager to go trick-or-treating.

"Huh?" Somehow I had fallen, too easily I think, into the slowest-ship-in-the-fleet role on this team.

"Come on, Angie." Marie picked up my purse and jangled my keys. "You drive. Halloween is less than a week away, and all the really good costumes might be gone."

Chapter 29

The animated conversation and caper planning continued as we piled into the minivan and headed downtown to Halloween Central. Details were fleshed out. Who would drive? Me. Who would get our tickets to the event? Gwen, she could get a discount. Etc., etc. Everyone took notes and tapped appointments into Palm Pilots. Old friends planning a holiday excursion.

What had happened here? Yesterday, I had three difficult best friends who didn't like each other, hardly knew each other, and who, with their rotten advice, had completely destroyed my life. Now I was driving my minivan loaded with truly wonderful best friends who felt very cozy with one another as we headed off on a mission to save me from ruin. So maybe it wouldn't work, and maybe after next Monday my son would disown me and I'd be part of Sacramento's latest scandal. But at that moment, I was feeling better than I had in years.

It was nearly five by the time we pulled up into the parking lot of Halloween Central, but the lot was full. The store was a huge warehouse that was transformed every year into a costume store for the month of October. It had everything: wigs, masks, period costumes, scary costumes, fake blood, fake vomit (though I'd proven myself very capable of producing abundant supplies of the fresh stuff if our caper called for it), and weapons. Halloween Central was *the* place to go for any kind of costume or disguise.

We were heading into the adult costume section when Jessica screeched to a halt.

"Oh, my gosh! It's him!"

"Him who?"

"*Him* him!"

Being the densest of the team, I rounded the corner and there he was: Ben Waters. I stumbled backward, my stomach queasy.

"Uh-oh. I know that look. Angie, put your head between your knees and breathe." Gwen pushed me down under a rack of fluffy petticoats and thumped on my back.

Marie peered around the corner. "Gwen, Jess, this could be a great opportunity! Help me think!" By now all of us were nestled under the pink-and-purple netting. "Darn, I wish I had worn something else! I don't look very attractive."

"Marie, what you have defies wardrobe. Here put on a little lipstick." Gwen pulled a shimmering gold lipstick case from her purse.

"What if I could . . . ? I don't know if he'll remember me. I'm always with Jack when I run into him."

"Marie, I can't imagine a man who wouldn't remember you." Jessica pulled a brush from her purse and fluffed out Marie's hair.

"Really? Thanks. So I maybe I could start piquing his interest somehow. But how do I bring up the scrapbook?"

"How about setting up the idea that to have a chance with you he's got to prove unquestionably that he's got what it takes, that he's a player in the sexual arena." Jess had developed an addiction for very racy romance novels lately.

"Or you could tell him that you're fascinated by men who have unusual collections . . ." Gwen handed Marie her atomizer filled with Passion.

"Or you could tell him that the number fourteen is your favorite number," I offered meekly.

Marie spritzed herself with a little of Gwen's perfume. "None of those sound quite right. But let's see what happens. I'm pretty good on my feet. And . . ." she tossed back her hair, giving us her steamiest look, ". . . on my back." Eat your heart out, Samantha Jones!

Marie stood up and took a deep breath. She pulled down her sweater and straightened her jeans. Then, with a final toss of her head, she walked slowly and rhythmically around the corner toward Ben.

They say that Mae West had an incredibly seductive walk and that men would hyperventilate watching Marilyn Monroe cross the street. But at that moment, I would have placed my money on Marie. Her walk was not the blatant "come and get some" kind of walk. It was subtler, more mysterious, and mesmerizing.

"Oh my gosh! How does she do that?" Jess whispered, as we crawled forward to watch the action. When Ben glanced up and saw Marie, he looked like he'd been unplugged. His jaw dropped, and I'm sure I saw saliva dribbling from the corner of his quivering mouth. He actually started panting, and his eyes were bulging in their sockets.

"Wow." Gwen, like the rest of us, watched in fascination. "Ladies, I believe we are witnessing the instinctual male libido, fully exposed. Pretty grotesque-looking, isn't it?"

Marie walked slowly closer and closer to Ben, each step adding to the beads of sweat gathering on his forehead. Closer, closer, nearly beside him. Then, seemingly oblivious to Ben's presence, Marie walked right past him. Ben snapped to and, tripping over himself as he turned, called out, "Excuse me, miss! Uh, Marie, isn't it?" His voice cracked like a thirteen-year-old.

The three of us scooted on our behinds beneath racks of caftans, cowboy chaps, and pirate suits, trying to get close enough to hear what was happening. But we couldn't. All we could do was watch the little dance of Ben scampering up to Marie, Marie pausing to drop a word or two before walking on, Ben scampering up to her heels again. This continued for several rounds. Ben looked ready to roll over on his back to get a tummy rub or pee on himself. Finally, Marie stopped and talked to him. She hit him with the full intensity of those gypsy eyes, and Ben looked close to fainting. After seven minutes or so, Marie made a clearly dismissive gesture. Ben scampered off and out of the store, looking like a man possessed.

Marie waited until she was sure Ben was gone, then rushed up to us, flushed and breathless. "I think we did it!"

"We did it? You did it, Marie! You were absolutely incredible! You should give lessons!" Jessica's voice indicated she was ready to sign up.

"I fully agree, Marie. You were simply amazing. Now

tell us exactly what happened." Gwen pulled out a pen to take notes.

"It was perfect! He started by asking about Jack, and I said that Jack and I are splitting up. I can't believe I said that. It just popped out. What if rumor gets back to Jack?"

"It's okay, Marie. Why would Ben tell anyone?"

"I guess you're right. Anyway, Ben lost no time in asking me out. I said 'No, thanks. I don't date married men.' Which is true; I never would."

Well heck, I wanted to scream, *neither would I if I'd known he was married!* I put my head down again, a combination of nausea and embarrassment this time.

"Then Ben told me he was getting divorced soon. I said, 'I've heard that story before, and I don't buy it.' He swore he had some very convincing evidence of his intention to divorce, but he wasn't certain he could show it to me. I said, 'In that case, I'm certain I can't go out with you.' By this time, the man was positively slobbering." Marie shuddered.

"The classic take-away. Men only want what they can't get easily," Jess observed.

Ugh! I tried not to think of just how very easy I had been!

"Well, it worked," Marie responded, "because then he declared he would show me the 'evidence' whenever I wanted. I told him I would be at the Halloween party."

"But I don't get it," I ventured. "Why would any guy with even minimal intelligence think you'd enjoy seeing that disgusting catalogue of recent conquests?"

My three friends looked at me incredulously, the depth of my naïveté seemingly limitless.

"Are you kidding, Angie? Intelligence has nothing to do with these things," Marie said.

"There are times when men think only with the brain below their belts," Jess added.

"Just look at Clinton. Rhodes scholar, college professor, president of the United States for God's sake! And even he couldn't keep his cigar safely in its humidor. Classic example of intellect defeated by the pull of the zipper." Gwen, heartbroken Democrat, shook her head and continued muttering to herself. " 'It depends on what your definition of the word 'is' is.' How stupid was that?"

"Anyway," Marie broke in, "I told Ben I would see him Halloween night and left it at that. What do you think?"

"I think our odds of that scrapbook being at Ben's house Friday evening just went up one thousand percent." Jessica beamed.

"Marie, you were brilliant." Gwen looked down at her watch. "Okay, the store is about to close. Let's get those costumes!"

The team scattered, launching into power-shopping mode. We met at the cash register fifteen minutes later, costumes in hand. All of us had chosen costumes appropriate to our roles in the caper. Marie, the seductress, had picked out a Cleopatra costume. Gwen, the distracter, chose a Morticia Addams outfit ("Beatrice wears one just like it every year. It'll drive her nuts that someone else will be in it—looking better than she does!"). Jessica, needing to climb and move stealthily, found a Catwoman costume. And me? Well, I figured I had to make sure that Ben didn't recognize me, and I definitely felt like I was going into battle. I picked out a GI Joe costume, combat boots and all.

*   *   *

The next week was an agonizingly slow one. I flipped from excitement and hope to anxiety and despair. The team held frequent conference calls to confirm details. If this was going to be a suicide mission, it would certainly be a well-planned one.

On Thursday, Tyler flew back into town, and we shared an early dinner together.

"Honey, you look so tired."

"It's just after cramming for the bar, then grinding on that project, Mom. It's been a bear! I've been living libraries for weeks. But I think I did okay on the bar, and the article looks good."

If past history was any indication, Tyler's "okay" meant brilliant.

"And I guess, Mom, it's just that I'm right on the verge of putting it all together, getting started on everything I've always wanted. It feels like it's been a long hard road, you know what I mean?"

I looked at my son, my beautiful, hardworking, sincere young son. And I realized that I couldn't, I *wouldn't* let him down. So sign me up as Extremely Motivated! Volunteer me to run naked through Walmart or catch bullets in my teeth! Whatever it takes, I'm ready!

"Mom? Are you okay?"

Tears were running down my face. "It's a hormonal thing, honey. It'll be fine, Tyler. Everything will be just fine."

Chapter 30

I hadn't thought of Halloween as The Big Day since the kids were little, but this one was the biggest. The benefit started at six, so I got home early to get into my costume. I had enlisted Jenna to help with the camouflage for my face.

"Mom, I really think you should have let me help you pick out your costume for tonight. I don't think this one is the dude magnet look you've been going for lately." She looked askance at the oversized battle fatigues accessorized with ammo belts. "And that green really isn't your color."

I didn't tell her that I was sure my dude magnet days were over. If I came through this one without ruining my family, I planned to become a nun, unless, of course, that required me to become Catholic or Buddhist, which I wasn't. Oh, well, if I didn't end up committing hara-kiri after tonight, I'd have plenty of time to research both religions and make an informed choice.

"Wasn't that the color of your hair junior year?"

"Maybe. Okay, so are we going for the Demi Moore GI Jane look? Or Sylvester Stallone, fierce scowl and all?"

"Stallone, I think." I needed all the bravado I could muster.

Jenna had printed some Rambo faces off the Internet to use as models. She covered my face with the base coat of grime-colored face paint.

"So, Mom, I've been so busy, I never got to ask you how your big date went."

"Um, it was okay. Not really my type though." Especially since my type does not include nasty, sleazy, weaselly blackmailers.

"Oh, that's too bad." Fortunately, Jenna is a dedicated artist when it comes to makeup and took her assignment very seriously. If she hadn't been concentrating so deeply on creating the perfect scowling eyebrows, I'm sure she would have been more suspicious about my answer.

"So you won't be seeing each other again?"

"No, I think not." Well, I would be seeing him in about thirty minutes. But if Jenna did her job, he wouldn't be seeing me at all. I figured I'd better change the subject before Jenna asked any more questions.

The ultimate sacrifice: "So, Jenna, what's been happening at work?"

"Oh, Mom, it's been incredible! I got to assist a liver transplant for a horse! I didn't even know they did those things, but what we did was . . ." And for the next fifteen minutes, I got a blow-by-blow description of the operation.

With my new angry-looking eyebrows, blackened lower lids, and cheeks covered with camo patterns, I was hardly recognizable, even to myself. As we finished up, tucking my hair tightly under the netted helmet, Marie entered in her gold lamé Cleopatra glory. She had painted her eyes dramatically, and an Egyptian-looking circlet held her long shining hair back.

"Wow! Mom, this is the kind of costume you should have picked out. You look fabulous, Auntie Marie! Totally hot!"

"Thanks, hon." Marie looked uncharacteristically nervous. "Well, we should be off then."

I slipped on my clunky, oversized combat boots and headed toward the door.

"Mom, you can't wear those shoes! Not for what you're going to be doing!" Marie and I froze. Caught already? "I mean, there will be dancing and everything, won't there? You may not even get asked to dance in that outfit, Mom, but you should be prepared. You can hardly walk in those boots. Here, wear these." And Jenna slipped off her fashionable black high tops.

"Thanks, sweetie. Good thought." I gave her a quick hug and escaped with Marie.

"Does she know anything?"

"No. But what if we get nailed for burglary? Do you think she could be named as an accessory for giving me her tennis shoes?"

"The more likely result of this evening is that Jack files for divorce. He was not pleased to see me going out all dolled up without him. And, of course, having been sworn to secrecy, I couldn't explain."

"Oh, Marie! I'm sorry!"

"Oh, Angie, don't worry about it! We're both being a little overly dramatic. Nothing bad could ever come out of this."

I hate when people say things like that. Like "you can't miss it" or "even a child could do it." Because I know I *can* miss it and, especially if it is related to technology, every child in the world has a better chance at success than I do.

Gwen and Jessica drove up just as we got to the minivan. This team might not have capered together before, but we were definitely punctual. The minivan had been cleaned in honor of our excursion, but everyone was too nervous to notice. The group was atypically quiet as Gwen navigated and I drove a cautious five miles under the speed limit. The last thing we needed was to be stopped by the Highway Patrol.

And where might you, uh, ladies be going?

See, officer, we are just going to steal back a lace thong that was taken from me by the husband of a local judge . . .

We parked in a long string of cars lining the lengthy driveway and eyed the Bennett/Waters house in silence. It was a huge house built on several elevations. We could see crowds of partygoers heading up the broad flight of stairs leading to the front door.

Gwen pulled out her hand-drawn map of the house and flipped on the overhead light. "Okay, the first floor, which is actually like a second floor in the front, has a dining room, living room, library, and kitchen. But it's actually the third floor in the back because of the cutout for the pool area."

"So the first floor is the second and the third floor." Jess sounded as if this made perfect sense to her.

"Exactly. Then the ground floor, which is the second

floor in the back and the first floor in the front, has a rum-pus room, a wet bar, and a pool changing area. You go down some stairs in the back to get to the pool itself."

"Are we going to be tested on this later?"

"Angie, please be serious. I've never been on the second floor, which is the front's third floor and the back's fourth floor, but I assume it has the bedrooms."

"And let us all pray right now that Ben doesn't take me up there to find his scrapbook." Cleopatra did not sound particularly enthusiastic about her assigned assignation.

"Where do you suppose he might be keeping it?" Jessica's question was a good one, but none of us could even come up with a theory. We synchronized watches—to Gwen's watch because she was the most adamant about its accuracy. The caper had officially begun. Collective deep breath, and we exited the car.

"Okay, I'm going around the back of the house and scope it out from the exterior. I'll meet you all inside." Jessica headed off, her Catwoman costume disappearing into the darkness.

"The rest of us won't enter together but scatter through the crowd. Angie, I'll go in first and find Beatrice. You should be able to recognize Ben, right?" I truly don't think Gwen meant to be catty with this last comment.

We melded into the ghosts and Tarzans and French maids trooping up the stairs. There seemed to be a loose reception line at the front door, six or seven people greet-ing the throng as they entered, which created a logjam that the fire marshal would have frowned upon. At the very end of the line, I spotted Ben, wearing a *Zorro* costume! Not Zorro! Zorro was my very favorite romantic hero as a child: *Out of the night when the full moon is bright comes the horseman known as Zorro.* Zorro was noble, dashing, brave, honorable—everything that Ben is not! How could such a scumbag have the audacity to wear that costume? Don't they give some kind of moral character test before allowing someone to be Zorro?

Who knows what sets off that fiery defiant streak in us? Rosa Parks's feet were just too darn tired to put up with racial discrimination anymore. Some guy in China didn't like a tank standing in his way in Tiananmen Square. My cause was certainly insignificant in comparison, but seeing Ben in that Zorro costume lit a fury in me that I'd not known before. The Warrior Maiden in me was awakened! It's a good thing that my GI Joe costume was not equipped with a flamethrower.

I wondered if Ben would recognize me as I made my way down the reception line. If he did, I was ready to take him out (I clearly recall that *Kill Ben* was one of our possible options), carving the big Z in his chest with his fake sword. But Ben didn't notice me at all. Marie was undulating down the line, and his slimy, dishonorable, uncouth attention was completely riveted on her. Zorro would have turned over in his noble grave.

Down the line I saw a woman that I assumed was Beatrice. It was a pretty safe assumption because A) she was in a Morticia Addams costume and B) the other Morticia Addams had glommed onto her per our plan. Gwen, looking much sexier in the same costume, had Beatrice in the verbal headlock of some legal debate already and was leading Beatrice to the other side of the room to duke it out.

I met up with Jessica by the jumbo shrimp, nabbed a

glass of wine from a passing waiter, and she reported on her reconnaissance mission.

"It's looking good. There's a pretty sturdy trellis up the back side of the house and decorative brickwork that will give me good handholds. I just wish I knew where the scrapbook was and where we need to be."

"We should know soon, Jess." We stood and watched our scripted play unfold.

"Okay, good, Marie has detached Ben from the reception line. And the Morticia twins are completely engrossed with one another. I think we're on track, Angie." Beatrice's face was turning beet red from the frustration of arguing with Gwen (I felt a twinge of sympathy for her, having experienced a similar frustration with my feisty, brilliant friend). On the other side of the room, Ben was equally red-faced gawking at Marie's cleavage (I felt no twinge of sympathy for him). Act One was going well.

And then, as in every play, the unanticipated plot twist emerged. A grandiose creature, straight out of "Flight of the Valkyries," swept into the room: Clarisse, followed by her faithful page Bob.

"Oh my gosh! Jess, look who just showed up!"

"Who? Oh, shit!" That was pretty strong language for either of us, but it fit the situation perfectly. "What if he recognizes you?"

"Jess, I have three pounds of camo greasepaint on this face. My own mother, if she were alive, wouldn't know me." Bob nudged Clarisse, pointed toward us, and started waving enthusiastically. "Shit, shit, shit!"

"All right, let's not panic, Angie. They'll probably just wander off and . . . Shit, shit, shit!" They were heading straight for us, Clarisse's massive armored bosom and pointed sword like a Wagnerian warship clearing a wide swath through the crowd in front of her, Bob following in her colossal wake.

"Shit, shit, shit!" I wish Jessica and I had a broader arsenal of obscenities at our disposal. I looked over at Gwen. Still arguing with Beatrice, she had caught the alternative scene unfolding, and her eyes were wide. Marie, heroically flirting with Ben, also arched an eyebrow in our direction. Women are excellent multitaskers.

Bob, looking positively diminutive next to his companion, stepped forward as if to speak but was swept aside by the Viking maiden's massive rump.

"Angie, how nice to see you!" Clarisse smiled grandly as if simply thrilled at the sight of me, undoubtedly because I looked so ugly in my oversized uniform and battle-ready face. "Bob tells me you are seeing someone. Is he here?" She looked around expectantly. I suspected she was ready to snag my new man, too, if there had been improvements made to the model.

Jessica recovered quickly. "No, he's not here actually. He's on a shoot in London." A shoot? Hard to tell whether Jess meant pheasant or film, but it sounded impressive. "Angie is incognito tonight because of all of the publicity their relationship is stirring up. You understand how invasive the media can be, don't you, Clarisse? Weren't you the object of their crude treatment not too long ago? Having to do with your husband's unfortunate demise?" Her eyes lasered into Clarisse defiantly. Jessica, on her bloatiest days, might be a third of Clarisse's weight, but in a test of wills Jess is a mega heavyweight.

The metallically clothed Valkyrie drew herself up and puffed out to Winnebago size. "There was no truth to those vicious stories. That incident of the fire department using the blowtorch to free me from the bathtub had nothing to do with . . ."

"Yes, yes, yes. But for your sake, we wouldn't want old gossip resurrected just because you happen to be seen with Angie, would we? Wouldn't it be safer if you just move along and ignore us for the rest of the evening?" Jess was a Chihuahua-sized pit bull, ready to chomp through Clarisse's iron breastplate.

"Yeah, but Angie . . ." Bob was silenced immediately by a nudge from Clarisse that sent him flying into the avocado dip.

"Of course, Angie, Jessica. Not a problem. We understand." With a huff, the mighty warship Clarisse turned and sailed on to another part of the room, little tugboat Bob still in tow.

"Angie?"

"Yes, Jess?"

"You married that guy, right?"

"Don't start with me, Jess. I'm not in the mood."

Marie and Ben were heading out of the room, her eyebrows signaling furiously for me to follow her.

"Here comes Act Two!" I chugged my wine, handed Jessica the glass, and hurried after them. They turned down a long gallery-type hallway (just as I suspected, art with no refrigerator magnets) and stopped in front of a set of double doors. Ben tried to maneuver Marie into a clutch, but she sidestepped it with running back precision. Defeated, he opened the door, and Marie followed him in with a last look over her shoulder, confirming that I was in position. I would owe her big-time for this one.

The plan called for me to wait sixty seconds, then pound on the door emphatically to break up whatever it was that would need breaking up by then. But how long is sixty seconds? My watch didn't happen to have a second hand to it. One thousand one, one thousand two . . .

"Hey, it's Mrs. Hawkins, right?"

I jumped. Who on earth . . . ?

"I recognized you when I came in. How is the reading coming?" It was Kevin, Mr. Information from the bookstore. I think he was wearing a costume, but I'm not absolutely sure. The kerchief on his head and the eye patch went so well with his tattoos and eyebrow ring that it could have passed as work attire for him.

"Um, Kevin, the reading's going fine." One thousand eight, one thousand nine. "But I'm kind of busy right now and can't talk."

"Oh, really? What are you doing?"

"I'm counting."

"Oh, okay." My counting seemed to make perfect sense to Kevin. One thousand seventeen, one thousand eighteen. "But I, like, really need to find a bathroom. Do you know where they have one?" One thousand twenty-eight, one thousand twenty-nine.

"I tell you what, Kevin. See those double doors? That's a bathroom." One thousand forty-one, one thousand forty-two. "So why don't you use that one? Only you may need to knock really loud first to make sure no one is in there, okay?" One thousand fifty-three, one thousand fifty-four.

"Sure. Thanks." Kevin trotted down the hall, and I scooted around the corner. He pounded on the door with an intense vigor inspired by youth and a full bladder. Marie came running out with Ben in hot pursuit. Kevin, strategically placed, got completely tangled up with Ben, giving Marie the lead by a furlong.

"Bottom drawer of the desk, right-hand side," she breathed as she passed me with impressive alacrity for a woman in full-length gown and high-heeled Egyptian sandals.

I hurried back to the main room to find Jessica in deep conversation with Russ, Mr. Mattresses Galore. Was everyone I had ever met in my life at this function? I gestured at her wildly, but all it got me was two attentive waiters with offers of canapés.

"Jessica? I need to talk to you."

"Why, here she is! Angie Hawkins, the woman I was telling you about, hon."

"Hon" was Russ's attractive thirtysomething wife who took one look at me and decided that her marriage was perfectly safe.

"Very nice to meet you, Angie."

"Yes, well, nice to meet you, too, and you have a delightful husband and all that, but I really need to talk to Jessica at this moment." I yanked Jessica's waiflike body across the room.

"The scrapbook is in the library, which is probably the fourth or fifth window across on this level."

"How will I know which?"

"Um, I'll go in there and blink the light on and off."

"Good plan. Give me five minutes to get in position."

Jessica worked her way through the crowd and scurried through the door.

"Angie? Angie Hawkins?" Shit, shit, shit! Who now? I turned to see the man with the dazzling smile.

"It's me. Tim, from the music store." Well, of course I knew it was Tim from the music store. Wearing a suit and tie, he was the only one in the room who looked even vaguely like himself or even vaguely like a rational adult.

"I guess I missed the part about this being a costume party. Though a suit for me could be considered a costume." He gave me an embarrassed grin. I swear every smile in this man's repertoire is outstanding.

"Tim, let me ask you this. I'm wearing six layers of truly ugly makeup, a helmet that hides my hair, battle fatigues that are seven times too large for me, and an assortment of fake weapons that are definitely not my normal fashion statement. Yet everyone seems to recognize me. What's with that?"

"Angie, you just have a way about you I guess."

Aw, that was sweet. Angie, snap to! You're on a mission. "So, um, Tim, is your wife here with you?" Maybe I could kill five minutes with Tim so that I didn't stand out suspiciously from the crowd as the only GI Joe ready to burglarize the house.

"Oh, I don't have a wife."

"Girlfriend then."

"Nope, not one of those either."

I was momentarily distracted from my mission. "Well, then who is it that you travel with all the time?"

"Travel with? Oh, you mean my business partner, Ralph? Trust me, Ralph and I are on a strictly platonic basis."

I was now *very* distracted. "So you . . . ?"

"I'm totally unattached? And what about you?"

Okay, so you may be thinking "what a goofball to be flirting with a man in the middle of a mission to save her honor and her son's career." But then again, you hadn't seen this guy's smile, had you? Don't be so quick to judge.

"Look, Tim. And by the way, I am totally unattached as well. We'll just need to take this up at another time, okay? Because I'm running on a tight schedule tonight and, well, I can't discuss it."

"Okay." He didn't smile this time, just looked deeply confused and a little hurt.

"Tim? I know I'm going to need some more music very soon. I promise I'll drop by. Will you be there?"

A hundred fifty watts, all at once. "Call first. I'll make a point of it." I hoped my smile matched his, but I'm not sure how happy a scowling Rambo face can get. Maybe a big grin just puts it into neutral; I'll have to check it out sometime. I turned and ran down the hall.

I entered the double doors, found the light switch, and blinked it furiously. I ran to the desk and, just where Marie had said it would be, found the infamous scrapbook. Tapping noises on the glass let me know that Jessica had made it up to the right window. With great difficulty—I've got to get back to those biceps curls—I opened the window. Jess climbed in.

"Did you find it, Angie?"

"Yep." Jess had the foresight to wear a backpack and we shoved it inside. She was halfway out the window again when we heard footsteps in the hallway.

"Quick, Angie, hide!" She pulled the window shut from the outside, and I dived under the desk. The doorknob turned and someone stepped into the room and walked toward the desk. My heart completely stopped and headlines flashed in front of me: *Matronly GI Joe Found Dead under Personal Injury Attorney's Desk.* The heavy footsteps came closer.

"Ben? Where are you, Ben darling?" Marie's voice came to my ears with the sweetness of a stay of execution. "Are you avoiding me, you big tease?"

"No. I just thought I heard something in here. I don't remember leaving the light on and . . ."

Marie obviously did something that shut him up completely. "Why don't we go join the party until we can have a little party of our own, hmmm?"

"Oh, yeah!" I heard his quick footsteps following hers. Bless you, Marie!

I ran to the window.

"Coast clear. You can go." Jess started climbing down. I waited just a few breaths, then ran to the door. No! It was locked! I was stuck! I ran back to the window.

"Jessica!"

"What?" She had just reached the ground.

"He locked the door!"

"Well, just come out the window."

"I can't."

"Why not?"

"Because I'm, I'm afraid of heights."

"Angie, this is no time to be fooling around."

"I'm not. I'm really afraid of heights."

"Well, it's only three floors. Just don't look down."

"Jess, they always say that, and it doesn't work! I can't do it!"

Jess let loose with a string of expletives that proved that we really could be creative with obscenities when the situation was dire enough. She started climbing back up the three stories. I must have looked pretty pathetic because she didn't punch my lights out when she finally reached the top.

"Okay, Angie, we'll figure this out. Maybe we can do it like skydiving . . ."

"You're going to make me jump?"

"Of course not! Angie, get a grip! I'm going to strap you to me the way they do with beginning skydivers. We'll climb down attached to each other."

"I don't think I can do that."

"Yes, Angie, you can. And do you know why? Because if you don't, I will be forced to thrash you with your ammo belts, which will probably put me in prison for a very long time and ruin my life, not to mention ending yours."

"Well, put that way . . ."

"Angie! Give me those belts!"

I handed them over and, fortunately, Jess used them to bind us together rather than to end my life. It was just like we were trying to fit into one of those horse costumes. I was the front end and Jessica was the rear end, the ammo belts buckled and wrapped around both of us. We scuttled backward like a disoriented crab to get to the window. Truly a Kodak moment.

The rear end of the horse worked its way over the sill first. "Okay, Angie, I'm going to place your feet on footholds as we go down. Got it?"

"Uh-huh."

"Angie, you have to keep breathing, okay?"

"Uh-huh."

"Okay, I've got you. Just step where I put your feet okay?

"Uh-huh."

"Ouch! Angie, dammit! Don't kick out with your foot! That was my nose!"

"Uh-huh."

Had I ever been this terrified in my life before? Nope, I don't think so. I was shaking and sweating and had a white-knuckle grip that could have crushed a ball bearing. In deference to the uniform and Jessica, whose face, due to shifting belts, was now pressed against my rear end, I did not pee in my pants. Four years later, we hit the ground, and I fell in a heap on the blessed, blessed ground.

"Angie? Are you okay?" Jessica had extricated herself and was speaking more gently now that she realized she wouldn't have to kill me.

"Jess? Let's never, never do this again, okay?"

"Okay, Angie. Let's get to the car."

By the time we stumbled to the minivan through the dark, Gwen and Marie were waiting for us. We jumped in with the precious backpack and sped home (going five miles under the speed limit of course). Everyone was talking at once.

"Hands of an octopus! Jack would have killed that guy . . ."

"She was so obnoxious! Five minutes of Beatrice would drive anyone to infidelity or the loony bin . . ."

"Camouflage does not work at all! Everyone knew who I was. And I saw the cutest guy . . ."

"She was petrified! I had to smash my face against her butt to keep her from falling . . ."

The chatter continued all the way to my house. We were Charlie's Angels, the Green Berets, Wonder Woman times four! We greeted the pups, and I uncorked a bottle of celebratory wine while Jessica opened the backpack. We stared in silence at Ben's odious scrapbook.

"It's got a lock."

"No problem." Gwen pulled out her fountain pen and flicked it open easily. "My older sisters kept diaries. It was the most practical reading of my junior high school education."

We opened the book and flipped through the pages, the sad little scalp collection of Ben's conquests. All those poor, unsuspecting women: #10, #11, #12 . . .

"Hey, it stops at #12."

"What?"

"I thought you said you were #13."

"I was! I am! It must be here!"

We flipped back and forth through the pages. No #13.

"He must have taken the last page out."

"Why would he do that?"

We looked at each other stunned, our celebratory wine untouched. There was no explanation. Gwen continued to turn the scrapbook pages slowly, as if willing the missing pages to appear.

"This was all for nothing then." My voice sounded very hollow and far away.

"Well, at least we saved #1 through #12." Jessica's voice was doing a very poor imitation of "the bright side."

"Angie, I'm so sorry. I don't know what to say." Gwen put her hand on my shoulder.

"Should we go back . . . ?"

"No, Marie. It's over." I looked up at my friends, who appeared to be as devastated as I felt. "So we tried but we failed. I truly appreciate everything you three tried to do for me. You were great, really. But it didn't work and, well, it's over. If you don't mind, I'd like to just be by myself now."

"Okay, Angie. But if you need anything . . ."

"No, Jess. I'll be okay." My three best friends slowly and reluctantly left. And then it was just me. I sat there for quite a while, totally numb, not really thinking at all. I got up and washed off the ferocious Rambo face only to find a very sad Angie face underneath it. I brushed my teeth, put on my pajamas, and climbed under the covers. Spud and Alli joined me, snuggling their beagle bodies in close for warmth. It was only then that I started to cry. And for yet another night, I cried myself to sleep.

Chapter 31

Early the next morning, Jessica's piercing voice found its way to my ears buried deep within my pillow haven.

"Angie! Wake up! Wake up! The others will be here soon!" Jess banged her easel and flipchart against the doorjamb as she struggled to get it through my front door. Déjà vu.

"What others? Jess, it's not even seven o'clock!" I groaned and opened just one eye to peer at her.

"I know, but we've got a lot of work to do. Gwen and Marie are on their way." She sounded positively chipper. This couldn't be the real Jessica, my absolutely NOT a morning person Jessica? And on this of all mornings, there certainly was nothing to be chipper about. No, it had to be part of some wacky nightmare I was having. I burrowed deeper into my pillows.

"Hey, Jess, I brought the extra markers you wanted. Angie, what are you doing still in bed?" Gwen looked like she had been up for hours, full of energy and purpose. She grabbed a wet washcloth, pulled off several pillows until she located my face, and threw the washcloth on it. "Here, this should help. I'll make coffee."

"Good morning, everyone! I brought muffins. Jack snuck out earlier and left them for us with a note. Then he took off again. Shall I heat them up in the microwave?"

I struggled to sit up and open my very puffy, cried-myself-to-sleep-again eyes. My kitchen/office/bedroom was bustling with the activity of my three best friends setting out cups and napkins, arranging chairs, taping up flipchart sheets. My wacky nightmare was beginning to smell like fresh-brewed coffee and apple cinnamon muffins. What on earth was going on? I decided to test this thought out loud.

"What on earth is going on?" Activity froze. Three sets of eyes stared at me, surprised by the question.

"Why, we're here to start working on contingency Plan B, of course. I've been kicking myself all night that we didn't develop one sooner. A good project plan always has a backup alternative, a fallback plan."

"Jess, it's not your fault. I know I was feeling so cocky that our plan would succeed that it didn't even occur to me that it might not." Gwen shook her head in self-disgust.

"Oh, I don't think anyone is to blame." Marie handed me my bathrobe. "But the fact of the matter is that we didn't accomplish our goal and now we only have forty-eight hours in which to do so. So we need to get to work."

"Get to *work*? Doing *what*?" My mournful wail rivaled those professional keeners who follow funerals in New Orleans. "It's hopeless, hopeless, hopeless! I'm a stupid,

stupid woman and a terrible, terrible mother! I can't do anything right! I'm totally worthless! I wouldn't be worth saving even if you could! Which you can't because it's hopeless, hopeless, hopeless!"

"Angelina! Shut up and sit up!" Jessica bellowed, a boot camp sergeant taking control.

I did as I was told. I shut up and sat up—even though my name is actually Angela not Angelina. I figured Jessica needed that extra syllable to achieve the correct tone of command. She whipped out her purple marker. "You are absolutely worth saving, and here's why: a) You're kind."

"And b) you have been a wonderful mother and c) you are very smart." This was from Gwen.

"And d) you are really fun to be with and e) you are a truly loyal friend," Marie added, Gwen and Jessica nodding their agreement.

The list continued, Jessica writing it all on her flipchart sheets, me sitting stunned and silent. There was a bit of wordsmithing. "You're funny" was edited into "You have a great sense of humor with excellent comic timing." And it took a while for them to agree on whether I was not only "open-minded" but also "adventuresome" (both stayed on the list). They liked my penmanship, my eyebrows, and my beagles—it was a very exhaustive list. And when the list was finished, we sat silently for a few minutes, all four of us a little teary-eyed.

"Thank you," I whispered. And my best friends nodded.

"So," Gwen moved to summation, "you see why we need to help you, Angie."

"Okay. Let's do it then." I hopped out of my pillow cocoon and put on my bathrobe. "Where do we start?"

"Well, let's resurrect some of the strategies we discarded previously and see if there is merit to any of them." Jessica flipped back to prior pages on the pad. "Here we go. 'Burn Down Their House . . .' "

We got to work, and half an hour later we were debating the use of Gwen's Colt 45.

"I'll have to review recent case law, but I think if it isn't actually loaded and if we don't go into the interior of their house with it . . ."

"Yoo-hoo! Can I come in?" Jack stood at my front door.

"Jack, darling, we're right in the middle of something."

"I know, Marie. I won't be a minute. I have something I need to give to Angie."

"Sure, Jack. Come on in." I figured we all needed a break from the morning's brain strain; the *Hold Them at Gunpoint* option was gaining alarming popularity. Jessica flipped back the pages to hide our notes.

"Here, Angie. This is for you. Open it." Jack's eyes were twinkling with anticipation. He handed me a sack that looked very much like a muffin bag but weighed almost nothing. He had tied a scrawny pink bow at the top. I untied the bow and tipped the bag upside down, and amongst the muffins crumbs that poured out was . . .

"Your special occasion thong! I remember that one! Darling, how on earth . . . ?" Marie leaped up and threw her arms around Jack.

"And the picture of Angie and the kids! Jack, you're a hero!" Gwen jumped up to join the hugging.

"How did you? Where did you?" We were all talking at once, hugging each other, hugging Jack. Jack, smart man that he is, enjoyed the hugging for a bit before he raised his hand in a practiced "order in the court" gesture to calm us all down.

"I simply followed Plan B and it worked perfectly." Jack beamed with satisfaction.

"You held them up at gunpoint?" Jess gasped.

"Held who up at gunpoint?"

"But, Jack, how did you get Gwen's 45? We don't own a gun, do we?" Marie looked worried.

"Gwen's what?"

"How on earth could you have known about Plan B?" Gwen demanded.

"You told me about it." Jack's face was shifting from beaming to baffled quickly.

"Gwen told you about it?" Jessica raised her eyebrow accusingly at Gwen.

"No, all of you did. Not Angie, but you three. Last night, remember?"

"How could we have told you about it last night?" Marie looked at our flipchart where Plan B was just be-ginning to unfold.

"Well, no, you didn't tell me outright. You hinted at it. You know, like hinting that you want me to empty the garbage."

"Did your garbage need emptying last night, Marie?" Gwen was struggling to get on top of this conversation.

"No, and it's not even our trash day."

"No, no, I don't mean garbage per se. But that hinting thing you women do. Like when you hint about what you want for your birthday . . ."

"But, Jack, my birthday isn't until April."

"And you're already hinting about what you want,

Marie? How very organized of you." Gwen was impressed.

"No, not your birthday . . ." Jack stammered.

"So does that make you a Taurus, Marie? It's a very sensual sign, and I can see it in your aura . . ."

"Stop!" I summoned as much command presence as possible given that I was wearing a fluffy bright pink bathrobe. I could see that this Abbott and Costello routine was about to bring Jack to tears. "Jack, just tell us the story in your own words. With no interruptions." I looked pointedly at my three best friends, but really, in this crowd what were the odds? In short, here is the story Jack was finally able to tell (through our frequent interruptions).

Apparently, Marie, Gwen, and Jessica, too upset to call it a night, had gone to Marie's house after leaving me. Jack was waiting up for Marie, and they blurted out the entire story of my romantic misadventure.

"Everything, Jack?"

"Everything, Angie." I blushed to match my robe as Jack continued. "How is it possible that a man can be so reprehensible? So despicable?" The rest of us bit our tongues, not wanting to shatter Jack's illusions with our numerous reprehensible, despicable guy stories.

So, after dissecting what could have possibly gone wrong with Plan A, Marie, Gwen, and Jessica had started berating themselves for not having a contingency plan, Plan B. Jessica had said that, since Plan A had employed feminine energy, Plan B would have to be masculine.

"That was their first hint, Angie. I found Jessica's yins

and yangs a bit difficult to follow. But since I was the only male in the room, I knew she meant that I was supposed to carry this out."

"Well, actually, Jack, women also have yang . . ."

"Hush, Jess! Go on, Jack."

Marie had then launched into a psychoanalysis of Ben Waters, which concluded that Ben would only be motivated to abandon his plan (and my panties) if threatened by emasculation.

"I thought she meant emasculation literally, physically, which made me somewhat squeamish. But Gwen pointed out that, to an attorney, the worst sort of emasculation is to be disbarred. She even cited every section and code Ben had violated and laid out a solid legal argument."

"You mean it's a felony to steal someone's underwear?" I asked.

"Not a felony, probably just panty larceny." Jack couldn't resist the pun, but his audience was too engrossed to respond. "But it is illegal to swipe someone's personal possessions, and the scrapbook proved that Ben had done that."

"Oh, you mean the scrapbook we stole from his personal possession?" Marie noted.

"Interesting point, Marie." Gwen's legal mind was now fully engaged. "But if that had become an issue, don't you think only Angie would have to plead guilty to burglary, Jack? And given the intent of the items stolen, surely she'd get a very light sentence."

I hated to interrupt this legal discourse, but I was confused and pretty nervous about the direction this was taking. A light prison sentence was not in my definition of a successful project. "So your legal strategy was based on me confessing to burglary?"

"Oh, no, Angie," Gwen said calmly. "It was based on Ben's intent to blackmail, which is definitely a more serious offense. Between the evidence of the scrapbook and your testimony in court, Ben could certainly be disbarred and probably prosecuted for his blackmail scheme."

"Anyway," Jack continued, "after Gwen developed the legal argument, Jessica pointed out that we only had forty-eight hours to implement Plan B, so we should start early in the morning. Clearly, I had my marching orders."

The team remained silent. Recognizing that I was the only one of us absent from the "hinting" discussion and therefore the only one legitimately clueless this time, I asked, "And, um, what exactly were those marching orders, Jack?"

"Well, obviously, to get up early, face Ben Waters man to man in a yanglike manner, and demand that he return your personal items or face the consequences."

A man on a mission, Jack had risen early, stopped by Starbucks to fortify himself with coffee and muffins, then headed to Ben's house. When Ben answered his doorbell, he was startled to see our yanged-up Jack standing on the front step muttering *Dirty Harry* quotes to himself.

"The coward tried to slam the door in my face. But I sold vacuum cleaners to get myself through school, and I've shoved my size thirteen through many a recalcitrant doorway."

Ben had then hustled Jack into his study so Beatrice wouldn't see him.

"He thought I was there about Marie. So it completely

floored him when I started talking about the scrapbook. I thought he was going to wet himself right then and there."

When Jack announced that we were in possession of his precious scrapbook, Ben had ransacked his desk. But the only thing he could find was the page for lucky #13.

"But, Jack, why wasn't that page with the others?" Gwen asked.

"Apparently, Angie's page was to be the grand finale in his presentation to his wife. Beatrice would have just hired Tyler; Angie was Tyler's mother. He thought that particular affair would make Beatrice feel especially 'invaded' and would clinch the deal for him."

Gosh, maybe I could put that on my résumé someday: *Had starring role in local blackmail scheme.*

"So then I demanded that he return Angie's things to me immediately. I told him we had her deposition ready and that we'd take it with the scrapbook to the California Bar Association and the DA's office first thing Monday morning. We would make sure that it went to jury trial so Angie would have the chance to tell all in court. She'd make a very credible witness and he'd be the laughingstock of Sacramento."

"Good psychological angle, darling," Marie murmured.

Yep, just great. I could just picture me, a matronly Monica Lewinski, giving blow-by-blow descriptions of my tawdry fling. I vowed silently that I would never, never, ever under any circumstances go out on a date again in my entire life.

Jack continued, "Well, Ben's not the sharpest crayon in the box. So even with all that, he waffled. The knockout punch was when I told him we would leak the whole story to the press this afternoon, kiboshing any possibility of his 'exclusive' with *People*, and making Beatrice so furious with him that I wouldn't bet five cents on his testicles' chance of survival." Jack blushed. "Pretty strong language, but it worked. He caved."

"Brilliant," Gwen whispered.

"I know I adlibbed on that last part. But you three had put together the basic plan and all the ammunition I needed. I was happy to be the messenger; I only wish I'd thought of it myself."

The four of us sat awestruck, staring at Jack like Jason and the Argonauts must have stared at the Golden Fleece. We were in the presence of a mythic hero, a man who a) actually listened to us, b) actually understood what we said before we understood it ourselves and c) actually acted appropriately from that information. A sacred hush fell over us; this was a life-defining moment. Jack started to squirm under our worshipful scrutiny.

Gwen came to first. "Jack, you are a very, very good listener."

"A man among men, really." Jess looked starry-eyed.

"You're wonderful, darling," Marie murmured, her eyes saying that she would show him just how wonderful he was as soon as they were alone.

"Really, Jack, how can I ever repay you?"

Jack took my hands in his and looked at me with his kind eyes. "Please, Angie, if you want to start dating, just tell me. I know a lot of very nice men. You deserve a lot better than you have gotten."

"Thank you, Jack." Then I started to cry. And everyone else started to cry. So Jack brought over some champagne, saying that if we were going to be all weepy, we might as well be drunk as well. We toasted to Jack and we toasted to Friendship and we toasted to Repossessed Lace Undies. We were toasting our way through our second bottle when Tyler and Jenna showed up.

"Hey, Mom! Everybody!" Tyler kissed me on the cheek, and I saw Jessica stuff the recently toasted undies back into the muffin bag. "What is this? A party?"

"Good grief, Mom. It's not even noon and you're drinking!" Jenna may have blue hair, but she does have a decidedly puritanical streak about certain things.

"Loosen up, young lady." Jack poured a glass for each of my kids. "We're celebrating friendship and reclaimed honor."

"So whose honor needed reclaiming?" Jenna is pretty swift, but Gwen interceded quickly.

"Tyler, didn't you have the big interview yesterday? How did it go?"

"Well," Tyler couldn't have had a more attentive audience. "I think it went pretty well. Judge Bennett is tough. She started quizzing me on some recent case law."

"Jespersen *v.* Zubiate-Beauchamp, I'll bet. That would be just up her alley," Gwen said.

"But it was a pretty weak ruling, don't you think, Gwen? Tyler, what do you think of it?" Jack relished a good legal discussion.

The three of them debated the merits of the decision while the rest of us sipped and smiled, pretending to follow the discussion. Jenna leaned over and whispered in my ear.

"Mom, Tyler was offered the job, but he declined it."

"What?" I spilled my champagne. Old habits die hard.

"Tyler? You didn't take the job? Why on earth not? I thought it was everything you always wanted!"

Tyler looked at me earnestly. "I thought so, too, Mom. But I've been doing some research on Judge Bennett, and I can't understand a lot of the rulings she's been handing down, especially the last few years. They seem to be totally politically motivated and flawed from a legal perspective, know what I mean? When I met the woman, she oozed with hostility, very self-serving and egotistical in a nasty way." He turned to the group as if addressing the courtroom. "Excuse my language, but she just struck me as a royal bitch. And I just won't work for someone I can't trust and respect. Mom, you taught me better than that."

There was a dramatic pause, then Gwen started the applause. We all joined in. We toasted Tyler and his good judgment, and most of us started tearing up again.

"Don't worry, Tyler. They've been doing that all morning. Now, young man, why don't you and I go somewhere so we can talk about other possibilities for your career. I've got some contacts that might be useful. Do you know much about model railroads?" And with that, Jack filled two glasses and motioned Tyler to follow him out the door.

"What's all this?" Jenna had noticed the pages of flipchart pages of *Angie Attributes* taped on the walls.

Jessica put her arm through Jenna's. "Well, these are some of the qualities that we think make your mom so special."

"You like her Christmas cards and Halloween candy?"

"Nobody has better. And look over there." Gwen pointed to another sheet. "We especially like her kids."

About this time, Marie decided that we had all been under so much stress that facials were in order. She ran over to her house and returned with New Zealand mud masks, which we applied, gray and grisly-looking, to each other's faces. Why is it that everything that's supposed to make you pretty starts out making you look so ugly? Gwen read aloud to us, passages from *The Big O* ("Okay, everybody get out a spoon. We're going to practice that last section."), and Jessica read our palms ("Angie, it says you're going to have a wild adventure with a midget on a Grecian island."). I don't believe I got out of my bathrobe all day. I spent it with Jessica, Gwen, and Marie, who helped me induct my daughter into the society of best friends.

Epilogue

Thanksgiving Day was cold and overcast, but it was toasty and bright in Marie's crowded kitchen. And this crowd included the people I love most in the world. Marie and Jessica were at the sink instructing Tyler in the manly art of perfect mashed potatoes while Gwen showed Jenna how to strain gravy at the stove. Jack and I set the table while Lilah (who had abandoned the celebration at Clarisse's as soon as she was able to pilfer the recipe for Double Chocolate Cream Cheese Brownies) poured wine for the kitchen crew and our guests in the living room.

Our guests were an assortment of significant and somewhat-less-significant others. Gwen had brought Wayne from San Francisco and Jess brought her fiancé whose name none of us could remember, even Jess, which might be a portent of some kind. But when my three best friends and I were able to sneak off in a corner, the big discussion was around the escorts my family had contributed this year. Jenna's date was her first "certifiable nondweeb," a veterinarian about fifteen years older than she is.

"Angie, do you mind that he is older?" Jess whispered.

"No, actually, I'd be more concerned if it was the reverse."

"Well, of course you would, Angie," Gwen inserted. "Because that would make him about seven years old."

"I've got to say that Tyler certainly is making up for lost time." Marie was referring to Tyler's date, Cindee, a curvaceous, sunny blonde who happened to be a lingerie runway model. "Do you think she's a keeper?"

"Well, she's a nice girl but . . ."

"But she's got the intellect of a Cabbage Patch doll," Jess noted.

"So she'll never grow up to be one of us," Gwen concluded. Since our Halloween adventures, being 'one of us' had become a badge of distinction. It meant something like brilliant, courageous, and resourceful, with extraordinary taste in choosing friends. Beyond the original four, only Jenna had been voted in as "one of us" so far.

"Well, let him enjoy himself," Marie said. "His mom certainly is!"

"Yeah, what's with your three dates tonight?" Jess asked.

"They aren't real, official dates," I protested. "Tim found himself in town unexpectedly, Jonathan's family lives in Wisconsin, and Tyler wanted to invite Eric. I figured we would have plenty of food." Tim was Mr. Music with the great smile. He and I had dated a few times, nothing serious and certainly no need for ironed sheets. Jonathan was one of the more attractive Igors from my gym who turned out to be a pediatrician (Lilah was making a play for him in the living room, and I wondered if she would have better luck with him than I had thus far.). Eric was a nice-looking attorney in Tyler's new office. I'd only met him once before, but Jack and Tyler were lobbying heavily for him. So maybe I wouldn't join the convent after all.

"Well, typically," Marie lectured, "it's okay to date several people during the same time period but not on precisely the same evening."

"But they're not dates!"

"I'm just warning you right now, Angie Hawkins," Gwen stated decisively, "that the Save Angie Crisis Intervention Team is no longer in service."

"No more running away from lechers in my high heels and Cleopatra gown." I doubted Marie would ever get over that one.

"And no more climbing down trellises with my face smashed against your buttocks." I suppose climbing will never be the same for Jess either.

I turned and looked all three of them squarely in the eyes. "But if I really, really needed you . . . ?"

And as one, my three best friends responded, "We'll be there."

**Turn to page 256
for a sneak peek at
IT'S NEVER TOO LATE TO BE A BRIDESMAID
Coming February 2006 from Avon Trade**

Want More?

Turn the page to enter
Avon's Little Black Book—

the dish, the scoop and the
cherry on top from
HEATHER ESTAY

About the Author

Heather Estay, author of *It's Never Too Late to Get a Life*, grew up as Heather Stevens in Denver, Colorado. She left Colorado to attend Stanford University in 1969 and has lived in northern California ever since. After graduating from Stanford with a degree in psychology, Heather pursued a variety of interests and occupations: transpersonal psychology studies, martial arts, meditation, house remodeling, creating desserts in a French restaurant, working for an employment agency, etc., etc. She finally settled on a career in commercial real estate, consulting for major corporations.

Heather has one nineteen-year-old son, Evan, and currently resides in Sacramento, California. *Little Black Book* caught up with her there for this interview:

Tell the truth. Are you Angie? No! Well, in a way, yes. Aren't we all a little bit "Angie"? Most of us are extremely intelligent in some areas and clueless in others. We can be very assertive in certain aspects of our lives, in our careers for instance. But then we might turn into whimpering cowards when dealing with our boyfriends or our mothers-in-law or our dental hygienists. (Personally, I'd prefer to go toe to toe with a mugger in an alley than request the saltshaker at a formal dinner party.) I don't think most of us are perfectly poised, perfectly confident, and perfectly competent in all arenas. (And if you are one of the few who are that perfect, who needs you?)

I did borrow some specific characteristics of myself to create Angie. For instance, like Angie I don't watch TV, not based on any philosophical grounds, I just don't think of it. I've never seen *Survivor* or *Sex and the City,* and I'm the only person I know who never saw one minute of the O J Simpson trial. Scary, huh? My friends and family are thrilled that I own a TV now (let's not tell them that I can't quite figure out how to turn it on).

I also don't read the local newspaper or any other newspaper regularly, and I don't watch the local news on television (which would require that I learn how to turn the TV on). So I've actually had the experience of meeting local celebrities and not having a clue as to their identity or significance (as it turns out, celebrities, local or otherwise, find this very insulting).

What else? I live with two beagles who coincidentally go by the names of Spud and Alli. My pups are much smarter, more beautiful, more attentive, more athletic and much better trained than the beagles in this book (they paid me to say this). They also swear that they do not snore or shed doggy hairs—yeah, right.

Angie and I are about the same age, and I'm divorced as well. But unlike Angie my divorce was seventeen years ago, and I've been a single mom ever since. I don't have a daughter, though I do have a son, Evan, who is a budding filmmaker, not a budding attorney. And yes, when Evan was sixteen, he dyed his hair fire engine red to match his car (Three years later, the car is still red but his hair is back to brown.)

Like Angie, I relaunched myself back into the dating world a few years back with less-than-stellar results. I've experimented with Internet dating, video dating, blind dating, and dating by blood type. (However, I've never inadvertently, or even advertently, gotten involved with a married man. I've done plenty of other dumb things in my relationships with men, but not that particular dumb thing.) I have yet to find Mr. Right or even Mr. Okay For Now. My mom says I'm too fussy; my friends say I'm too independent. Personally, I think I've read too much Jane Austen and Charlotte and Emily Brontë (and you know what great love lives these authors had.).

What about Angie's friends? Are they based on real people? The Save Angie Crisis Intervention Team? No. They're composites of dozens of women I know and probably dozens of women you know.

But I've had many friends over the years who are—how shall I say it?—"difficult." You love them, but you can only handle them in small doses. (Of course, I am not referring to any of my current friends, who are all absolutely perfect in every respect. If you don't believe me, I'm sure they would be happy to tell you so themselves.) And I've always had a very diverse circle of friends. The only thing many of my friends have in common is me, and the fact that they all seem to find me a little "different" (which I choose to view as a compliment). I like it this way. They expose me to a wide variety of life perspectives and experiences, and help me be more multifaceted and open. I suppose it is odd that some of my very best friends have never met one another. Maybe at my funeral . . .

So the entire plot is made up? None of it really happened? Well, no. Actually some of the bizarre plot twists and totally outrageous scenes actually *did* happen to people I know. However, I will never, under penalty of bikini waxing, reveal which parts are based on fact.

Reality is definitely stranger than fiction. If you need proof, just get a small group of women together with a couple of bottles of wine. I can't possibly live long enough to write all of the funny, heartbreaking, ludicrous, charming, weird, and just plain nasty stories I've heard over the years. Now that people know I'm writing, I hear even more of them.

How did you come to write this book? Well, Vicodin and Valium played a large part, as did my older sister. Here's what happened: I had fooled around writing a couple of chapters and e-mailed the drafts to my sister, Laurie. That same night, my back went into massive muscle spasm, and I was completely incapacitated. Laur called the next day to tell me she loved the chapters, she had laughed out loud, and she thought that I really should keep writing. Here I was, flat on my back, full of painkillers and muscle relaxants. How the heck could I keep writing a book when I couldn't even move?

But Laur (being a bit bossy as older sisters are wont to be) insisted that I lie there and think about it, work out plot details, flesh out the characters. And that's what I did for two whole weeks. I lay in bed and muttered the dialogues to myself, visualized the characters, and scribbled notes on a couple of lined pads. This activity probably saved my sanity, and by the time I could sit up and get on my laptop, the book was nearly finished.

Writing the second book, vertically and without drugs, was much more difficult.

You've never had any formal writing training or experience. What made you think you could write a book? I didn't know I *could* write a book. But then again, I didn't know I *couldn't* either. Does that make sense?

Years ago when my son, Evan, was twelve or thirteen, I read a book that was supposed to be humorous about women and golf. When I finished it, I said, "Heck, I could have written a funnier book than that." Evan looked me straight in the eye, took dead aim, and said, "But you didn't, did you, Mom." Ouch! The truth hurts, and our kids are particularly good at nailing us with it, aren't they? (Another good argument for birth control.)

Of course, he was right. I had talked about and thought about writing for many years. But I'd never actually done anything about it. The wonderful thing about being "women of a certain age" is that we've fulfilled all the basic requirements: raised the kids, done the career, etc., etc. And now, what have we got to lose by trying something new? Following a dream or maybe just an interest? Actually, this is probably true at any age. But it's much more apparent in our late forties or fifties. And if we don't love what we are doing or who we are by that age, do we want to continue the next twenty, thirty, or forty years in that same unfulfilling rut?

Were you surprised that your first book was published? Yes and no. I had researched the whole process, how a manuscript is supposed to look, finding the right agent, writing query letters, etc. Within all my research, it became clear that *statistically* it was a long shot that the book would ever see light of day. But we're not statistics, are we? We're individuals. It's not that I was confident that the book *would* be published. But I didn't put any "confidence" in the naysayers or dismal statistics either. I merely did the next thing that was supposed to be done.

So what's next for you now? Well, my second book, using the same characters as in *It's Never Too Late to Get a Life,* is done. Next, I'll be trying my hand at writing mysteries. My friends and family have supplied me with a list of all the people they would like to see offed in these next books. It's a pretty extensive list, so it looks like I'll be writing for a while. . . .

Curious about what happens next with Angie and the Save Angie Crisis intervention Team? If you enjoyed *It's Never Too Late to Get a Life,* you'll love the sequel, *It's Never Too Late to Be a Bridesmaid.* Here's an excerpt, coming February 2006 from Avon Books.

You know, if I were a sitcom, I would have been canceled by now. Honestly, some expensive-suited, high-powered studio exec with a nervous eye twitch would have taken one look at the last two months of my life and deep-sixed it:

"No, no, no! Too many plot lines! She can't have everything in her life go wrong at the same time. One problem per week, that's the limit. And what about the romance? She's single, right? They'll be expecting romance. And whose bright idea was it to throw her in jail? Too farfetched. Totally illogical. Yank it."

And of course, he would have been right. Prior to two months ago, my rap sheet consisted of exactly one parking ticket in 1988 written by an overzealous meter maid. So landing in the slammer (don't you love the sound of that?) was perhaps not my next most logical step. But then again, who would have predicted that Martha Stewart's next venture would feature horizontal stripes rather than pinstripes? (I have nothing against Martha Stewart personally. But anyone who thinks it's festive to float lotus blossoms in a toilet bowl really should be incarcerated for her own safety.)

Also prior to that week I went out of town, the "plot lines" in my life were pretty straightforward and simple. When I left that Thursday everything was just fine. I had the prospect, if not yet the reality, of a few eligible men in my life. My daughter Jenna was self-confident and single. My son Tyler was rational and grounded. Gwen was smart, Marie was nice, and Jessica . . . okay, so Jessica was never quite normal, but at least she was her own Jessica-self when I left. But all of that normalcy unraveled like a skirt hem caught on a nasty nail the minute I left town.

Maybe my world had gone berserk *specifically* because I was gone for that week. Maybe my absence disrupted the cosmic balance like a celestial trade deficit destabilizing the equilibrium of my personal universe. Then again, maybe not. All I know is that by the time I returned the following Friday, plot lines, lifelines, phone lines, fine lines, panty lines—all sorts of lines had gone totally out of control.

As for the romance, well, most of my love life has been as scintillating as a back issue of *Field and Stream,* with a few scenes from *Monty Python* thrown in. So really it should come as no surprise that my romantic life was not proceeding exactly as planned or as hoped. Whose does?

Maybe my life lately is too bizarre for a sitcom, and maybe it could never qualify for a romance novel (then again it's not a horror movie either, so I should be grateful). Actually, it would probably play better as science fiction. Can't you just hear Rod Serling introducing this?

"A town. An ordinary town, like Sacramento. Where friends are friends, men are available, and children behave. But imagine: Angie Hawkins, middle-aged, postsoccer mom, leaves this ordinary town for one brief, innocent business trip. And when she returns, she enters . . . The Twilight Zone."

Honestly, you know you're in trouble when a jail cell is a welcome haven. Beam me up, Scotty . . .

Shelley Dunnigan

HEATHER ESTAY lives in Sacramento, California, with her two Beagles, Spud and Alli. Her previous experience writing fiction included several wildly unsuccessful singles' ads and many almost-believable budget variance reports. *It's Never Too Late to Get a Life* is her first novel. If you don't buy this book, it may be her last.

HEATHER ESTAY

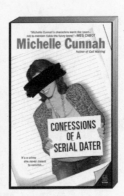